Shattered

A Novel

K.B. ANDREWS

Pink-Tree Publishing

*This book is for my readers
and anyone who has ever
been
fucking shattered.*

1
The Bucket List

"I can't believe you're going to leave me alone all summer. I mean, what am I supposed to do while you're gone?" I complain while rubbing sun tan oil over my legs.

Katie turns her head to face me. "What do you mean? What about Nick?" she asks, shading her vibrant blue eyes from the bright light of the sun.

My clenched teeth sends a bout of pain surging through my jaw as I hand her the oil. "Fuck, Nick. He's a douche."

She sits up and takes the bottle. "Did he do something?"

I lean back with my eyes closed and sigh, letting the sun warm my skin. "Yeah, he cheated on me with Holly. Can you believe that?"

She snorts. "Holly? Seriously?"

Holly is the slut in our group of friends, or should I say

Katie's friends. She's nothing more than an acquaintance to me, and an annoying one at that. She's never invited anywhere, but shows up everywhere.

I feel the vein in my forehead begin to pulsate. "Yes, Holly." I sit back up and reach for the mixed drink on the table between us. "No boyfriend, no best friend. Worst summer ever!"

"You could come with me." She flashes me a wide smile.

I take a deep breath. "You know I can't. If I could, I would be there in a second. I can't get the time off work."

She leans back and brushes her hands over her legs, the sand that clings to them falls away. "So? Screw that dead-end job. This will be the summer of a lifetime if you come with me. Who wouldn't want to go spend the summer in Miami?"

"I would die to go on this trip with you, but I can't afford it either," I mumble, avoiding her gaze while scanning the ocean in front of me. I watch as two children pull away from their parents, giggling and splashing in the water while the couple share a secret moment together. The man places his hand on the woman's hip and pulls her against him, whispering something in her ear that causes her to laugh and kiss him. A spike of jealously runs through me.

"You know I could—"

"You're not paying for it, Katie. Seriously, you know how I hate to be your charity case."

She lets out an exasperated sigh. "You're not my charity

case. You're my best friend, and I like doing things for you. What do you say?" She flashes me 'the smile' which has always gotten her everything.

"No. It's too much." I relax back into my seat, pulling my long, dark hair out from under my neck, the strands clinging to my damp skin.

I honestly don't know what I'm going to do with my summer. Katie is my best friend. We've never spent more than a couple of days away from one another since grade school. She's always been here for me to lean on and talk to.

I'm shy, and don't fit in easily. I never have. I keep to myself, preferring to read a book than go out drinking where I'm forced to socialize with people.

She is the complete opposite. She's outgoing, fun, lovable, and gorgeous. Not only is she all of those things, she's also rich. I mean, *slap your grandma rich*. I've always wondered why she picked me as a best friend.

We met the day she sat at my coloring table in kindergarten and we've been like sisters ever since. If it wasn't for her, I never would have stepped out of my bubble the small bit I have.

"What do you say to dinner and dancing tonight since I leave in the morning?" Katie asks, interrupting my thoughts.

I roll my head to the side to look at her smiling face. Her blonde hair is tied in a knot atop her head, and her blue eyes sparkle whenever the sun shines against them.

"I don't know. I was just going to order some pizza and read a book."

She sits up fast and throws her legs over the side of her chair, spinning around to face me. "Oh, no you don't. I'm going to be gone for three months. You're spending the evening with me even if it kills you."

I groan, "but dancing? Can't you pick something else?"

She rolls her eyes before letting out a long, dramatic sigh. "Fine, how about we have a night in. We can order some takeout, do makeovers, watch a movie, and get drunk."

I point my index finger at her. "Now you're talking my language." The corners of my mouth turn up as I stand. "Let's get packed up so we can get this party started."

"You're such a dork. Who in their right mind would rather hang at home than go out and have fun?"

"Um, do you know me?" I fold up my towel and stuff it into my bag, ready to be in the comfortable confines of my apartment.

I WALK OUT of the bathroom to find the coffee table in my living room littered with junk food. "What is all of this? I said *dinner*, not a months' worth of junk food and a dentist bill."

She laughs as she walks up to the table, looking over the selection. "Too much?" Her brow wrinkles with the question.

I walk closer. "Let's see, Chinese, Tai, Pizza, Pringles,

popcorn, Twizzlers, Raisinettes, and *what* is that?" I lean over the table to get a better view.

She frowns at me like I'm a crazy person. "That's Dirt Cake. Seriously, you don't remember Dirt Cake?"

I feel the corners of my mouth pull up. "Oh, yeah. God, I haven't eaten this since we were in grade school." I pick up the small container of chocolate pudding covered in crushed up cookies with gummy worms, and remove the lid. I sit down on the couch as I grab a gummy worm and pop it into my mouth.

"Really? I eat it at least once a week." She flops down beside me and grabs the other container.

"Once a week? You're as bad as a kid." I laugh.

She shrugs. "What are we watching?"

I turn to her with a smile. "You *know*."

"Dirty Dancing?" She grins widely.

I nod, causing her to cheer and bounce up and down with excitement. "God, we haven't watched this movie in forever." She pulls the blanket over her legs to get comfortable.

I turn on the movie and crawl beneath the blanket with a carton of Chinese food. "I know, but I bet we can still quote the entire thing."

She looks at me with a dead serious expression, brows pulled together and lips pooched out. "Nobody puts baby in a corner," she quotes the movie.

I laugh and smack her knee. "You should see your face when you do that," I say around my high-pitched giggle.

She quirks her eyebrow at me. "Really? Think you can do a better job?"

I shake my head as my laughter subsides. "Nope, you're on point."

She breathes on her nails and wipes them on her shirt. "See, I knew those acting classes would pay off."

I snort.

She quickly turns to look at me. "What?"

"How much did those classes cost you?" I ask, not turning away from the TV.

"I don't want to talk about it." Her voice has now taken on a bitter edge that I find amusing, but I do my best to keep the taunting inside.

THE MOVIE IS ALMOST over when she turns to me and asks, "so, have you talked to Nick since you found out?"

I feel my good mood leave, as if the simple question sucked it right out of me. "A little. He says he was drunk and didn't know what he had done until the next morning."

She rolls her eyes. "You're not going to take him back, are you?" Her voice is shrill, cutting through me. I feel like she's berating me, like she doesn't approve. Of course she doesn't.

I don't look at her. I can't. I'm too embarrassed. I mean, who would do that?

I would. I would do that.

"I don't know, Katie. It's hard, you know?"

"What's hard? You deserve better than that asshole. Dump his ass!"

I finally look over to see the anger etched on her face. "Then what? Be alone? I'm not like you. I don't have a line of men waiting to date me."

"Who cares? And you do have a line of men. You just won't look at them or take the first step."

I start picking at the skin around my fingernail, not wanting the confrontation. "I can't. I'm just not that person. I've never been Ms. Popularity like you."

She levels her eyes on me. "You have to start seeing what I see in you, Jo. You're more than you think. You're a great person. You're my best friend. You deserve to get out of here and see the world. You deserve to meet a great man and fall in love. Have you ever been in love?" she asks, knowing the answer to that question.

I scoff. "That stuff is only for books and movies."

Her jaw drops before she stands and walks over to my desk. She grabs a tablet of paper and a pen.

I follow her with my eyes. "What are you doing?"

She plops back down beside me. "We're making a list of all the things you're going to do this summer. When you see me again, I want all of these checked off."

"What if I just check them off without doing them?" I challenge.

She removes the end of the pen from her mouth. "I will know. I'm serious, Jovi. While I'm gone, I want you to live.

Live like I'm here with you." She points the end of the pen at me and it seems like a light bulb has come on above her head. "No, live like I am dead and you're living for the both of us. You know how much I expect from life so you better fulfill each and every one of these things."

I laugh it off. "Fine. Make your stupid little list," I say, knowing damn well that I probably won't do half of it.

"Number one: Dance in public, like nobody is watching. Number two: Kiss a stranger."

I quickly turn my head toward her. "Really? That's just gross."

She smiles but keeps writing. "Number three: take a trip — for fun, not work. Number four." She studies me. "Fall in love."

"How am I supposed to fall in love in three months? It will take me that long just to work up the courage to talk to a guy."

She ignores me and continues to think out loud. "Number five: have a one-night stand."

My eyes roll automatically. "Oh, come on. Now you're just making fun of me."

She laughs but keeps writing. I don't even bother paying attention anymore.

AN HOUR LATER, the list is complete and lying forgotten on the coffee table under the copious amounts of junk food. We each have a fruity drink in our hand while she applies my makeup.

"I *said,* close your eyes," she grumbles while trying to give me the smoky eye look.

"I can't," I complain while fighting with my eyelid to stay shut.

"You're making a mess with all the blinking you're doing."

"Ouch, it's in my eye." I pull away from her and desperately rub my eye, hoping to flush out the black powder.

I finally look at her and see the wide smile she's wearing. "What's so funny?"

She shakes her head and covers her mouth to try and stop her laughter.

"Show me," I demand in my serious voice.

She reaches for the mirror and holds it up for me to see.

There is black eyeshadow all over my cheek, my eye is red and bloodshot, and the makeup is smeared clear across my face. I can't help but to laugh.

"Add, 'learn to apply makeup' to that list." She points at me before sitting back and taking a drink.

I grab a tissue from the box on the end table and wipe at my face, trying to rub off any makeup I can. "I'm going to miss this."

She gives me a sad look, looking up at me from beneath her long lashes while sticking out her bottom lip in a pout. "It's only three months, and you know you can always come along."

I shove the thought away with a wave of my hand. "I can't do that. Sure, you can pay for the trip, but who's going to pay my bills here when I get back and don't have a job?"

She smiles, showing me her straight, white teeth. "You can move in with me. Why we were never roommates is beyond me. Why didn't we get a place together?"

"Because I was determined to support myself, and I knew that would be impossible living with you. Especially with your accountant that pays everything for you. Do you even know what a bill looks like?" I tease her.

"Yes, I've seen the stacks you have lying around here." She sticks her tongue out at me.

I laugh and take another drink before asking, "so what does Seth think of you being gone for three months?"

She begins picking at her perfectly polished fingernail. "I broke up with him," she says casually.

"What? Why? You two have been together for almost a year."

She pulls her legs under her and turns her body towards me. "Because this is it, Jo. I'm not being held back. This is the vacation of a lifetime. I'm going to watch the sun rise over the beach with a drink in my hand. If I find a sexy man I want to take back to my hotel, I'm going to take him back to my room. I don't want my real life holding me back. I want to be free to take every opportunity that comes my way." She holds her arms out at her side with a fluid movement like she's prepared to take on the world.

Hearing her confession only makes me feel even

more shut off. Why can't I be more like her? She's completely free, living however she wants without letting the rules control her. I'm afraid of everything. I've never been able to take a chance the way she does.

My head falls back to rest against the couch. "God, I'm so jealous. Why can't I be more like you?"

She scoots closer to me, pulling my head against her shoulder as she wraps her arms around me. "I love you just the way you are, Jovi. But I admit, you could come out of your shell a little." She pulls away slightly to look into my eyes. "Promise me you will try this summer. Try to check everything off this list."

"Katie, that list is just silly. How will doing any of those things help me?"

"Come out of your shell little by little and I *promise*, by the end of the summer, you'll be ready to pack up and leave this city behind you."

"Have a one-night stand?" I question with my voice void of emotion.

She laughs. "Well, start with one of the easier ones."

"Which is?"

She thinks it over. "Eat something spicy?"

I let out a chuckle. She knows me too well. I don't eat spicy food.

"Kiss a stranger? Dance in public?" She shakes my knee. "Seriously, the next time we see each other, I want this list crossed off. Promise me that you'll try. Just try."

The amount of love and friendship shining in her bright blue eyes makes me waver.

I smile. "Okay, I promise."

She claps and bounces up and down. "Good, this will be the best summer of your life, even if I'm not around."

Just the thought of her not being around for the summer makes me want to cry. She's the only person I hang out with. With that, on top of breaking up with Nick, I'm looking at one lonely summer.

She looks at her watch before standing. "I should get going. It's late and I haven't packed yet."

"You're leaving in five hours and you haven't packed yet?"

"Na, I figured I'd pack all night and then sleep on the plane," she says as she slides her feet into her flip flops.

I follow her to the door. "Be safe and call me. A lot!"

She spins around and pulls me in for a hug. "I love you, Jo."

"I love you too."

She releases me and gives me a longing look. "This will be great, you'll see."

I roll my eyes. "Yeah, yeah. When you get back, you owe me a mani/pedi day for the horrible summer you're about to inflict on me."

She points at me. "Deal. Mani/pedi's, dinner, and drinks."

I let a silent laugh fall from my lips. "Have fun, and

don't catch any diseases!" I holler at her as she makes her way down the hallway.

She holds up her middle finger just before she rounds the corner to the elevator.

I giggle and close the door.

I walk through the apartment and turn off the lights, not bothering to clean up our mess. Tomorrow is Saturday, I'll have all day to clean up.

I wash my face free of the makeup she'd caked on, and pull on some pajamas before crawling into bed.

I turn off the light and settle beneath the blankets. I hope that she is right. I hope this is the best summer of our lives. I need a break. I need to get out of my shell a little, but it's so hard when I feel like I have to force myself to do something as simple as going to a bar and talking to strangers.

If it wasn't for her, I'd probably be the crazy cat lady.

2
The Game Changer

I WAKE IN THE MORNING AND ROLL FROM BED, HEADING straight to the shower in hopes of getting rid of this hangover.

I don't ever drink much. I only had three of whatever it was Katie made last night, but they were strong. I have a headache the size of a Buick.

I take extra-long in the shower. When I step out, the small space is filled with steam as the moisture beads up on the mirror and white tiled walls. I walk back into my bedroom and dress in a pair of black leggings and a baggy sweatshirt. I pull my wet hair up into a bun on the top of my head, and go in search of food. I'm not going to do anything today but clean up my apartment. No point in trying to be presentable.

I walk into the living room and see the coffee table still home to our leftover junk food fiesta. Crumbs are scattered across the white carpet, and the white and cream colored couch is ruffled and covered in blankets. I roll my eyes and pass it by, opting to get some sustenance before tackling *that* project.

I make myself a bowl of cereal, and take a seat on the couch as I'm turning on the TV. I flip through the channels aimlessly until something catches my eye. My finger stops pushing buttons as I hear what the news announcer is saying.

"Flight 108 departed from Los Angeles at five A.M. this morning heading for its Miami destination. Unfortunately, something went terribly wrong." It flashes to a fiery plane crash.

The hand holding the spoonful of cereal freezes on its way to my mouth as I watch the story unfold.

The announcer continues to explain what happened to cause the crash, but my ears suddenly stop working. I can't hear a word. I can only see the images flashing across the screen.

There is nothing left of the plane. Its torn apart metal lies in heaps across the scorched earth. There are rescue teams rushing to put the fire out while the words, *"No found survivors"* run across the bottom of the screen.

All I see is fire and smoke. The earth that was once flat and green is now a massive divot that holds the burning plane. People are rushing to the scene to assess the situation while news teams surround the nearby area. The entire place is covered in flashing red and blue lights.

My ears ring and my chest burns from lack of oxygen as I sit watching this horrific event, still unable to hear a word they are saying. And I don't really care because my best friend was on that flight.

Without thinking, I hurriedly set the bowl on the coffee table and rush to my room to get my phone. I look on the bedside table where I normally put it, but it's not there. Frustrated, I toss the blankets off my bed in an attempt to locate it.

"Please God! Please don't let her be on that plane!" I pray out loud.

When I come up empty handed, I run back into the living room and throw everything off the coffee table. Everything spills and seeps into the white carpet.

It isn't here either. I turn and throw blankets and couch cushions onto the floor. I don't care about the mess. All I care about is whether Katie was on that plane.

With everything thrown from the couch, I finally find it. It must have fallen between the cushions last night. I grab it and frantically swipe the screen to see twenty missed calls.

I ignore them all and dial her number.

"Hi, it's Katie. If I don't answer I'm probably lounging at the beach or too busy becoming famous to talk to you. Leave a message and I'll call you back. Maybe." She giggles over the recording.

I fall to my knees, clutching my phone in my hands. My

eyes land on the fiery scene that still plays on the TV, not quite believing what I'm seeing. But it's like my entire world has been shattered. All I can hear is my heart pounding wildly while I desperately try to take in enough oxygen.

HOURS LATER, I'm lying on the floor, tears still streaming down my face. The crash is still playing, and I can do nothing but watch it.

Over, and over, and over.

It's like I feel the need to punish myself because it was *her* who'd been stolen from this world and not me.

It should have been me.

She makes the world a better place. She's kind and loving. She's outgoing and would do anything within her power to help anyone in need.

I do nothing but stay shut up in my apartment, avoiding almost everything.

I'm still clutching my phone to my chest, unable to move. It's rung several times now, but I haven't even attempted to answer it. I can't. I'm in shock. My best friend was on that plane. She's gone. I won't see her at the end of the summer. I won't see her ever again.

The pain hits me like a powerful wave, crippling me. It's like I'm floating in the middle of the ocean and the waves are unrelenting, beating me up and pulling me under until I almost pass out. It only releases me just to do it all over again. My heart pounds in my chest erratically. My breathing is shallow, all but stopping. My headache has only gotten worse with the crying, and my lungs burn for much needed oxygen. Oxygen I can't seem to breathe in because my lungs feel deflated. It's like everything around me is in slow motion as I'm wracked with grief.

My whole body is numb with pain. It's all I can feel.

Loss.

Loneliness.

Pain.

Why did this happen? She should be having the time of her life right now. She should be lounging on a beach, being handed mixed drinks by sexy waiters. She should be sending me Snapchats of the fantastic view. She should be texting me to play *screw, marry, kill*, with every guy that passes her. But instead, she's gone. Taken out in a fucking plane crash.

She would have to go out dramatically. That thought makes me giggle just a little. She was always dramatic. A sudden fit of hysterical laughter washes over me and it makes it even harder to catch my breath.

I barely hear the knock on my door over my laughter before my mother rushes to my side. I see her above me and I see her lips moving, but can't hear what she's saying. All I hear is the ringing in my ears while the blood rushes through them.

She drops to her knees and pulls me against her chest. Suddenly, the laughing stops as everything speeds back up.

"She's in shock. Help me get her to bed," she tells someone.

The fit of laughter has now turned to full on tears. They quickly overfill my swollen, puffy eyes and run down my hot cheeks.

My dad picks me up and places me softly on my bed. My mom pulls the blankets off the floor and covers my shaking body. I don't know why I'm shaking. Am I cold? I don't know, I can't feel anything but heartbreak.

Once again, I see my mom move above me, but my eyes are flooded, causing everything to look blurry.

I curl into a ball and close my eyes that sting with the threat of more tears. She lays down next to me and curls herself around me, rubbing my back and brushing away the hair that is stuck to my wet cheeks.

Finally, feeling a bit of comfort, I fall into a deep, dreamless sleep.

I WAKE in the morning and look around my room. Something is different but nothing has moved. There's this pressure in my chest that feels like it's going to crush me, like my heart is in a vice that just keeps getting tighter.

With a sharp pain in my chest and a dull ache in my stomach, I force myself from bed. I haven't had anything to drink in over twenty-four hours, yet somehow, I need to use the bathroom.

After washing my hands, I debate on getting in the shower, but decide against it. Instead, I head towards the kitchen for a glass of water.

As I'm walking down the hallway I hear my mom and dad talking from inside the kitchen. I pause to listen to what they are saying.

"Should I call a doctor? She slept like a rock all night long, but every time I would wake to check on her, she was still crying. I didn't even know you could cry in your sleep," my mother says, worry evident in her normally soothing voice.

"She'll be fine. She lost her best friend. She's going to hurt. She just needs time to adjust," my dad replies.

Hearing his words makes my heart ache. I take a deep breath and push myself forward. I don't acknowledge them as I walk straight to the sink. I take a glass from the cabinet and fill it to the brim with water, all the while, feeling their eyes on me.

I chug the glass like I can't get it in fast enough. When I turn around, breathless, they are both watching me, frozen like statues.

"How are you feeling, Jovi?" my mom asks.

I shrug and fill the glass again. This time, instead of devouring it all at the sink, I take it to the table and sit down. "My head hurts." No doubt from all the crying from the day before.

"I'll get you some Tylenol," Dad says as he pushes away from the table.

My mom sits down beside me, placing her hand over mine and rubbing slightly. "I know you don't want to hear this right now, but Katie's body has been recovered and—"

"No! I don't want to hear it." I jerk my hand away and lean back in my seat, crossing my arms over my chest like a spoiled child that's in trouble.

My mom flinches from my harsh tone. She places her hand over her heart and closes her brown eyes like the stressful situation is just too much for her to handle. How does she think *I* feel?

"Here you go, sweetheart." Dad hands me the pills and I wash them down with a long drink.

"I'm sorry for yelling, Mom." I stand with my glass of water. "It really means a lot to me that both of you are here." I turn away before they can reply, and walk to the couch. I sit down and look around the room.

The mess I made looking for my phone has been cleaned up. Even the spilt cereal that I shoved off the table has been scrubbed from the carpet. The glass coffee table is completely clean, all but that damn notebook.

"I'm serious, Jo. While I'm gone, I want you to live. Live like I'm here with you. No, live like I am dead and you're living for the both of us. You know how much I expect from life so you better fulfill each and every one of these things."

I lean forward and pick up the list. I start flipping

through the pages. There are three whole pages of things to do. How could she even write this quickly?

I don't bother reading over them. Leave it to her to guilt me into this list. If I didn't know better, I'd think this was her plan all along: force me to be uncomfortable, to come out of my shell, force me to live.

Tears sting my eyes again.

I have to live while she's gone.

I have to live for the both of us now.

And without a doubt, I have to do this damn list.

IT'S BEEN three days since Katie's plane crash, and I haven't left my apartment since. I'm not living. I'm doing the opposite. I have watched Dirty Dancing continuously, eaten nothing but dirt cake, and read the list over and over.

I only leave my bed to use the bathroom. It's like all the energy has been sucked from my body. I can't force myself to live on without her. There is a constant pain in my chest that makes me wish I could quit breathing, but because life is the bitch it is, it allows me to live in constant pain.

My parents have gone home, but they come by to check on me every day because they know I won't answer my phone.

I can't.

I don't want to talk to the many people that have been calling to tell me how sorry they are. I can't deal with my reality right now. So in an attempt to ignore it all, I pull down the shoebox in my closet that is filled with pictures and trinkets of our favorite memories.

I set the box on my bed and look at the lid. We made this box when we were in eighth grade. The pink construction paper glued to the top reads *"Jovi and Kate's B.F.F. Memory Box,"* written with silver glitter paint. It's old and tears fraying the edges makes it look worn.

I take a deep breath and pull off the lid. I pick up the stack of pictures resting on the top. I look at the first picture of us. It's from last summer when we took a cruise. We're looking directly into the camera, wearing big smiles that highlight our sunburnt cheeks. I flip to the next one to see a picture of Katie from the same trip. But in this one, she's leaning over the side of the ship, puking into the ocean from being seasick.

I giggle and set the pictures aside. I pick up a piece of folded up paper and open it up. It's a note from grade school. It reads,

Jovi, thanks for sitting by me at lunch today. If you wouldn't have sat there, Tony Matthews would have. And as we all know, he eats like a starving hyena, and I wouldn't have been able to keep my lunch down. My stomach thanks you.
Have fun in gym!
Your BFF always,
Katie

I laugh to myself and fold the page back up. I continue digging through the box and find random postcards from the trips we have taken together over the years. I find matchbooks with guys' numbers written on them, guys I probably promised her I'd call and never did. There are sea shells from our trips to the Key's and other pictures of us throughout our years together, but it's the unfamiliar hot pink envelope in the bottom of the box that steals my attention.

I pick up the envelope and open it to find cash and a note.

Jo, if I know you, you are probably missing me like crazy right now. If this is true, take this money and join me on the trip of a lifetime. But don't wait too long! You don't want me to get to all the hot guys before you can get here!
Love your best friend,
Katie

My eyes fill with tears that stream down my cheeks, landing on the letter.

When could she have put this in here? Did she sneak into my room when we had our last night together? I clutch the money to my chest, unsure of what to do.

I can't believe she did this.

My eyes fall to the list she made that's setting on my bedside table, the one I've read over a hundred times now. I look over her cursive handwriting. "Take a trip— for fun not work."

I look at the money and note in my hands.

I know what I have to do. I have to take Katie's trip.

I have to cross off everything on this list.

I have to live for us.

THE WEEK PASSES by too quickly for my liking. Before I know it, it's Katie's funeral. I pull on a black dress and heels and check myself over in the mirror. I pull my hair off my neck and into a sleek bun. I look at the makeup that lines my vanity, makeup that Katie probably bought for me.

"Learn to apply makeup," I say, remembering her words.

I turn on my phone and open the Youtube app to look for makeup tutorial videos. I laugh at myself. This is crazy. How is a Youtube video going to teach me to do my makeup?

In an attempt to try, I watch the video and repeat the steps until my face is painted. I look at myself in the mirror.

My usually plain face is now covered in blush, eyeshadow, eyeliner, and lipstick. It doesn't look like I had a seizure doing it either. It's not the best, but I consider it a win!

I reach into my bedside table, pulling out the list, and write, "Learn to apply makeup". Then I check it off.

"One down, Katie."

I'm numb through the entire funeral. I have to be. I can't let myself feel all the emotions that are threatening to crash down on me right now because they would cripple me. My chest feels tight, my heart literally hurts, and my lungs burn, needing to take in more oxygen, but I can't give them anything more than what I'm already giving them.

Holding my breath is the only thing that is keeping me from bursting into tears. My body feels dragged down and tired, even though I've slept more this past week than any other. I have to force every step I take.

I have to force everything.

I sit quietly in an uncomfortable chair and stare at the forest-green carpet. I can't look around at her friends and family falling apart. Just thinking about having to talk to someone about the good times Katie and I shared brings tears to my eyes. I don't want to talk about her like she's gone. Because to me, she isn't gone. She lives on with me every day.

As everyone files out, I accidentally look up at the big framed picture of her. Her blonde hair is hanging down around her face in loose waves, her blue eyes are bright and happy, and she looks completely carefree, the way she always did. A sob makes its way up my throat as my eyes flood with tears.

My dad puts his arm around my shoulders and leads me out of the door and to the car. I slide into the backseat and rest my forehead against the window, watching everyone in their black clothes cling to one another on the sidewalk. Tears flow from their red, bloodshot eyes down their flushed cheeks. I see her mom fall to her knees in a grieving fit while her dad tries to pull her back up to her feet.

My heart cracks just a little more.

3
Kiss a Stranger

MY DAD FOLLOWS THE LINE OF CARS TO KATIE'S childhood home. With the plane crash, her parents opted to have her cremated, meaning no cemetery. I couldn't be more relieved. I can't imagine my best friend spending the rest of eternity there. She belongs with her family.

We pull up to the big, brick house, and park in the circle drive. I lean over and look out my window at the house that's home to so many of my childhood memories. I stayed here as often as I could growing up. I don't know if I can set foot in there and survive the assault of unwanted sadness that is sure to come.

My dad opens my door and I step out of the backseat. "Are you sure you're ready for this?" he asks, taking my arm in his.

I shake my head but push on.

"Your mom said to call if you need anything. She wanted to be here today, but I think a part of her feels like she lost a daughter of her own."

I hear his words but I don't feel them or respond. Right now, I'm only thinking about pushing forward. The last time I was here was Christmas. We had dinner with Katie's family, and sat around the tree opening gifts and singing carols while her mom played along on the piano.

The closer we get to the red front door the harder my heart pounds. I can hear it in my ears above all else. My breathing is shallow, and my head begins to swim.

I pull my arm away from my dad, and my feet stop moving.

He turns to face me. "Are you okay? Do you want to leave?" Concern is etched on his face, creating deep wrinkles to form around his blue-gray eyes.

I shake my head. "No, I just need a minute. Please, go ahead. I'll be in soon."

His head tilts to the side, silently asking if I'm sure, but I nod him on.

He joins the many other people walking inside while my feet begin to move backwards, away from the door.

When the last person has walked in, I turn and head into the back yard. I walk across the lush, green grass and sit down on the old wooden swing hanging from the big oak tree.

I grasp the ropes tightly in my hands, holding on for dear life. I'm still dizzy as tears begin to swell in my eyes.

"I'm sorry, Katie. I don't know if I can do this without you. You were the brave one, not me," I whisper.

The back sliding glass door opens, drawing my attention up. A guy with blond hair walks through, holding two glasses. I try not to stare, but he demands my attention. His hair is long on top with a part on the side that fades down to a buzz. His blue eyes are bright, but they also seem clouded and bloodshot like he's had to deal with too much stress today as well. He's tall and lean, but looks strong as he walks closer to me.

I turn and look around the yard, wondering if he's going to have both those drinks himself or if there is someone else out here that I didn't know about. I see nothing but the perfectly manicured lawn and flower beds.

When I turn back to look at the blond god, he's standing right in front of me, towering over me as he holds out a drink.

His closeness makes me buzz as I look up into his deep blue eyes. "Thank you," I all but whisper as I accept the drink he's offering.

He nods without a word and leans his shoulder against the tree. I raise the glass to my nose and smell the alcohol before taking a sip. It burns my throat as it goes down, and I cough.

I hear him chuckle beside me and I look at him, smiling weakly before turning back to my drink.

Neither of us are talking, we're just enjoying the quiet. His proximity makes my heart hammer away, making me feel nervous, but also calming me somehow. Just having someone with me makes me feel a little more at ease. Someone who understands my need for space.

I tip the glass to my lips again, swallowing the contents in one big gulp.

"You may want to take it easy with that stuff. It's a little strong." His deep, raspy voice cuts through the silence, almost making me jump.

"That's exactly what I need right now." I look into the bottom of the empty glass, wishing for more. Above all else, I just want to be numb right now, just a few minutes to escape the pain and anguish of this day.

He walks a few steps closer and kneels down at my side. He places his drink on the ground and pulls a flask from his jacket pocket. I hold out my glass while he pours me a little more.

After he pours my refill, he takes his place at the tree again.

I want to ask who he is, but I don't even have the strength to talk at this point. The whole week has been weighing on me, this day the most.

I feel like the weight of the world is resting on my back and shoulders like the sculpture of Atlas. The only difference is, I'm not big and strong. I'm not brave enough to take it all on. I'm small and weak. I feel the weight of it all pressing down on me, ready to make me collapse. I'm tired of the stress, the loneliness, and the pain.

I swirl the amber liquid in my glass and finish the drink. I stand to go inside so I can find my dad. I can't stand to be here anymore, surrounded by her childhood home and happy memories.

When I stand, the guy leaning against the tree stands upright. I feel dizzy as I walk across the uneven ground to him. I hold out the empty glass for him to take.

"Thank you. I really needed that."

He offers up a breathtaking smile and nods before taking the glass.

Kiss a stranger. I hear it like it was whispered in the wind.

Without thinking, I close the distance between us in two steps, and press my mouth to his. A spark shoots through me the second we touch. I place my hand on the side of his angular jaw as our lips and tongues glide against the others.

I can taste the liquor on him, and his deep, rich scent surrounds me.

I pull away and look up at his bright blue eyes. Something is brewing behind them, but my embarrassment has gotten the best of me so I don't stick around to ask him anything. I turn and quickly walk away from him with heat radiating from my face and ears.

"You're lucky I love you, Katie," I whisper as I walk into the house through the sliding glass door.

The elegant house is littered with flowers that have been

sent by their loved ones, and every square inch of the place is occupied by a grieving guest – a constant reminder of loss.

I try not to think too much about them as I navigate through the rooms, searching for my dad. I finally find him talking with Katie's father, George, in the study.

"Hi, cupcake," he says when he sees me walk in.

I offer a sad smile as I go to stand at his side.

"How are you, Jovi?" George asks. His blond hair is disheveled and turning white, and his blue eyes are surrounded in deep wrinkles, making him appear older than he really is.

I shrug. "Not so great. How is Mrs. Hansen holding up?"

I see his eyes water, but he refuses to let the tears fall. "Not very well. She came home and went directly to bed."

I place my hand over his that is resting on the desk. "I'm sorry for everything."

He nods and quickly pulls me in for a hug. "You're welcome here any time. Please visit, you're like another daughter to us."

I step away and nod. "Thank you, Mr. Hansen."

"Are you ready to go?" Dad asks me.

I nod before he tells George goodbye. As we turn to leave, George calls out my name.

"Oh, Jovi."

I spin around to face him. "Yes?"

"I have something for you. I was going to give it to you

at the funeral, but I couldn't stand to leave my wife." He reaches into the inner pocket of his suit jacket and pulls out something shiny. He holds it in the palm of his hand.

I step closer and see a silver necklace with a small glass charm. Inside the charm is swirls that looks like sand.

"We used some of her ashes to have this made for you. We knew you'd want to carry a piece of her with you."

Tears are building up on the brim of my eyes, threatening to overflow and spill down my heated face. With a shaking hand, I reach out and take the necklace. "Thank you so much," I say, almost in a gasp.

I hold the charm in my hand with the chain dangling down between my fingers. It's so beautiful. In the center of the charm looks to be a small, pink flower with the ashes swirling around it. I clutch it to my chest as I lean in for a hug.

He squeezes me close. "I meant what I said. Please come visit. I don't think Mary could stand losing you too."

I pull away and wipe my tears, looking up to see him wiping away his own. "I will," I promise.

WHEN I GET HOME, the first thing I do is grab Katie's list and mark off *"kiss a stranger."* I smile to myself as I do so. This list is a piece of Katie. The only piece I have left.

The booze I drank earlier has caused a relaxing feeling to wash over me. It's also given me a false sense of bravery.

I look over the list to see if there is anything else I can check off tonight.

"Eat spicy food. Get a haircut I'd never get. Dance in public." I laugh.

I'm not feeling up to eating, and maybe I shouldn't pick a random haircut after I've been drinking. But dance in public? That I can do. Or at least, try to do. I've already taken the first step anyway by drinking enough to not care.

I look up at the white ceiling tiles. "I hope you're up there laughing your ass off right now."

I toss the list to the side and move toward my closet to change. I pull on a black, sequined dress and pair it with high heeled ankle boots. I let my hair down and it flows around me in loose waves. My makeup still looks okay, so I head towards the door.

Twenty minutes later, I'm walking into the dance club that Katie always dragged me to. I figured this would be better than a bar. Clubs always have a mass of people dancing. Maybe nobody will notice me.

I head straight for the bar, and try blending into a darkened corner while the multicolored lights flash around. When the bartender finds me, I order a drink and sit down to work up the courage I need to get out on the dance floor.

My nerves keep bubbling up, but every time they do, I wash them down with more alcohol. My eyelids feel heavy by my third drink, and I feel myself relax even more. I'm watching everyone dance when *Sorry* by Justin Bieber comes on. Katie loved him. I know this is my sign.

I take a deep breath and push away from the bar. I'm practically shaking as I walk under the flashing lights, towards the swaying bodies. I find an area in the back, in a dark corner where there's less people, and start to sway my hips. I feel completely awkward and out of place, but I have to do this.

I have to finish this list and make her proud. I close my eyes so I can't see the faces that surround me, this makes it much easier. I listen to the loud music pulsing through the club and try to envision that it's just me and Katie dancing in my living room. My arms seem to rise automatically as I spin and dance around to the beat of the music.

A smile forms on my face as I twirl beneath the flashing lights. My heart feels lighter somehow and my skin warms like I'm standing in the sun light. An unexpected tingling forms in the pit of my stomach that makes me open my eyes. I see the blond mystery guy from earlier.

He's standing on the opposite end of the dance floor, but he has his sights set on me. His eyes rake over my body unabashedly and his sexy lips, that taste delicious, begin to turn up in a smile. I feel embarrassment wash over me.

My body stops moving as he draws closer. I never would have kissed him earlier if I had known that I would have to see him again. As he corners me, my heart pounds harder.

I stand unmoving on the crowded dance floor, watching as he stalks toward me. Our eyes never break their connection as he closes the distance.

I can't hear anything over my own heart as he stops directly in front of me. His chest is practically touching mine as I look up at him. I think he's going to say something, but instead he leans in and kisses me. His lips collide with mine and his tongue snakes out to taste me. I open willingly for him. The kiss we shared earlier was only the tip of the iceberg. He gives me so much more than he did earlier.

His hands cover either side of my face while he tastes me. I grab onto his shirt and pull him closer, getting lost in this feeling he's stirring inside of me.

What am I doing? This isn't me. But maybe that's the point. Maybe I'm changing.

His hands fall to my hips, and he moves against me, never breaking the kiss. After a few more seconds with his mouth against mine, I pull away and look up at him.

His blue eyes have darkened and his lips are red and glistening from our kiss. I want to ask him why he kissed me, why he's dancing with me, how he found me, but I don't. I don't want to ruin this moment with talking. I just want to feel, be carefree, even if only for a short time.

I turn and rub against him. His fingertips dig into my hips as he dances behind me. I feel him grow hard, and it shoots a wave of pleasure low in my belly that makes my flesh sticky.

I want him.

But I don't know him.

I don't even know his name.

The perfect person for a one-night stand.

I push the thought away immediately. I can't do this.

I shake my head, trying to clear it of all the confusion as I pull myself from his grasp, walking off the dance floor.

I can feel him watching me as I get further away, but I don't turn back.

I need a drink. I need to clear my head. All this stress and heartache is getting to me. I would never make these decisions if I was in my right mind. Hell, I wouldn't even be here right now.

I kissed him earlier. I did it for the list, but I wasn't expecting to actually feel something.

Seeing him again, in the darkness of this club, not knowing his name, only makes me want him more. He's dark and mysterious, and that makes him dangerous. Something I've never been attracted to before.

I order a strong drink and throw it back the second it's in my hand. I set the glass on the bar and when I turn around, he's standing right beside me. He looks over at me with something in his eyes I can't place.

He leans in close and his scent drifts my way, causing this fog to settle over me. "Why'd you walk away?"

I swallow down the fear that's bubbling up my throat. "I'm just confused."

His eyes bore into mine like he's searching for something. "What confuses you?"

"Everything. Why this happened. Why I'm here. Why you have taken such an interest in me."

He gives me a lopsided grin. "I took an interest in you because I can see you're in as much pain as I'm in. I thought we could keep our mind off it awhile, together."

His hot breath blowing across my neck causes a shiver to run through me, goosebumps break out across my skin.

"I don't even know who you are."

He waves down the bartender and motions between the two of us. "And I don't know who you are."

The bartender places a new drink in front of us both. I pick it up and take a drink. "And that doesn't bother you?"

He shakes his head before taking a drink. "Nope, the only thing that bothers me is how you obviously want this too, but you're avoiding it...or too afraid of it."

I feel like he's insulted me. My back straightens and I square my shoulders. "I'm not afraid of you."

He finishes his drink and turns to look at me. "You're not afraid of me, but you are afraid to let yourself feel free for a while."

I throw the rest of my drink back and turn my whole body in his direction. "That's what you think? That I'm so uptight that I can't even dance with a stranger?"

He shrugs. "I bet you wouldn't know how to have a good time if it kicked you in the ass."

My eyes squint before I rise to his challenge. I grab his hand and pull him back out to the center of the dance floor. When I turn to face him, he has a big smile that's spreading across his face.

I place my arms around his neck and pull myself against

him. He grabs hold of my hips and keeps me close. His hand snakes around my back and rests just above my ass. We're locked into some sort of staring competition, so close that our lips are almost touching. His hot breath blows across my skin, and the way he's moving against me feels too good. I find myself closing my eyes, enjoying the reactions he's causing in me.

I'm completely unprepared when his lips touch mine. My eyes pop open before I relax and give into him. He's pushing me and I know it. He wants to prove to me that I can't have fun and be free. He's going to push me to my limit, push me until I cave and run away. But I won't. Not this time.

This time, it's for Katie.

With a surge of bravery, I let my hand fall from his neck. It glides over his chest and down to his growing erection. I brush against it and the moment I do, his lips still as he sucks in a hissing breath.

He breaks the kiss, and with the darkest eyes I've ever seen, says, "what do you think you're doing?"

I offer up a flirtatious smile and take a step back. "Living in the moment. Letting go. Having fun. Don't tell me you're the one that's afraid now."

He pulls me back against him. "Don't start a fire you don't know how to put out, sweetheart."

I bite my bottom lip and look into his dark eyes. His words only egg me on. "I have no doubt in my firefighting capabilities."

Without a second thought, he takes my hand and pulls me behind him, leading me out the door and around the building to the back alley.

When we round the corner, he spins me around and pushes my back against the wall. He presses himself against me with his hands holding firm at my hips. "How sure are you now, princess?"

"I'm no fucking princess." I wrap my hand around the back of his neck and pull his lips to mine forcefully. His tongue dives inside, twisting with my own and further fueling my passion. His hands travel my body, pulling me closer, teasing all the right places. I'm practically dripping with need for him, for this man I don't know.

His hand runs up the outside of my thigh and under my dress, pushing the thin material out of his way. He grabs my panties, pulling at them until the lace rips and falls at my feet. The thin lace being pulled so roughly burns the skin of my hips, but the pain somehow mingles with pleasure, creating this yearning to form in the pit of my stomach, something I've never felt before.

I've never had sex like this. It's always been slow and causal. Not rough, hard, and animalistic. When he breaks the kiss, I open my eyes to see him standing in front of me. His chest is heaving, his jaw is flexed, and his eyes are as black as night.

In the darkened shadows of the alley, he looks like something else altogether. He isn't the cute guy that leaned casually against a tree earlier today. No, now he's dark and dangerous, like a beast that stalks its prey in the night, taking exactly what he wants from me as he's fueled with lust and desire.

Seeing him flip a switch like that only makes my toes curl with anticipation. I want this…with *him*. I've never wanted a man this much in my whole entire life. And I've never wanted this kind of sex. But with him, I want it all.

His dark blue eyes never leave mine as he unfastens his belt. The metal clanks in the dark, causing the tiny hairs on my damp skin to stand up straight.

It's like he's afraid to take his eyes off of me in fear I will run away. He pulls a condom from his pocket and opens it with his teeth, the action raw and gritty.

But I'm not about to run. Not this time. This time, my body is getting exactly want it wants. I will no longer allow myself to run away because things frighten me or get too intense.

Instead of running like my brain is begging me to, I reach out and unbutton his jeans before sliding my hand down the front. The moment my hand comes into contact with him, he lets out a hissing breath and his mouth crashes against mine, owning every part of me.

He breaks the kiss as he grabs my wrist and pulls my hand away from him. Lowering his jeans over his hard erection, he slides the condom on.

Suddenly, he steps toward me, pressing his chest against mine as he grabs my thighs and lifts me up, pressing my back against the wall.

He positions himself at my entrance but pauses. "Last chance to back out."

I roll my eyes. "Shut up and fuck me."

As those last words escape into the night, he slides deep inside, filling me to the brim. My nails bite into his shoulder as an audible gasp leaves me.

I've never heard that sound leave my lips before. It sounded straight pornographic, so much so that his dick twitches inside of me. He leans back, looking over my face with a sexy but smug grin playing on his lips. He cocks his head to the side. "I think someone likes it rough," he says, pulling out and thrusting back inside of me.

I bite the inside of my cheek to keep from calling out and drawing a crowd.

"Did you even know that about yourself?" Slowly he pulls out, and quickly hammers back into me.

I don't want to talk. I can't. Right now, all I can do is feel. And I need him to do that. I need to know the feeling of being pushed over the edge of the earth. I need to know what it's like to spin and spin until I'm still and the world is spinning around me. I need the feeling of being shattered into so many pieces, there's no possible way of collecting them all.

I move in for a kiss, and as if he knows what I need, he moves his mouth to mine, giving, taking, completely fucking dominating me.

He holds my hips tightly, so tight I bet I'll have bruises tomorrow. But that's also something I need. I need the reminder of this moment on my skin so that when I wake up, I'll know it was real, that it happened.

He moves in and out of me forcefully, hitting that exact right spot. His hands tour my body, squeezing my hips, waist, and breasts. His tongue slides against my own before he bites my lower lip, causing a searing pain to flood over me. And even though it hurts and I can taste a faint tinge of blood, it causes my release to rise and shatter at its peak.

My nails dig into his shoulder blades, and I let out whimpers and moans until I feel him shudder his own release with a growl. He pumps hard into me one last time, so deep I scream in pain, but pain is something I've come accustomed to. It's a part of me now. And it's changing me.

4
Eat Something Spicy

MY LEGS ARE STILL WRAPPED AROUND HIS HIPS, AND HIS chest is pressed against mine. He looks up at me, and his blue eyes are shining again. They are a clear blue with green undertones. Just staring into them sets my body ablaze, especially now that I know he can press all the right buttons inside of me.

I don't even know this man, but he's the only person left that's ever challenged me to feel and to be free. I want to know more about him: his name, where he's from, why he was at Katie's parents' house today. But I'm almost afraid that getting these answers will break the spell for me.

Staring into his eyes as his chest rises and falls quickly, his hot breath blowing against my face, it's all beginning to feel too intimate, a place I'm not willing to go. I push against his chest until he pulls out of me and places my feet on the ground.

He turns his back to me while he pulls off the condom and tosses it into a nearby dumpster, and I straighten my dress.

I can see his arms moving, like he's positioning himself back into his pants, and then I hear the zipper on his jeans. I know he will be turning around any minute now, and the alcohol is wearing off. My face feels like it's on fire. I need to get out of here before he turns around and we have to have some kind of awkward conversation.

I quickly walk back around the building as quietly as I can before he sees me. Once I'm no longer in eye shot, I pick up the pace and rush around to the front to hail a cab.

Katie must really want me to have this one-night stand, because the first cab I see stops, and I jump inside.

In a rush, I tell him my address. He shifts the car into drive and hits the gas. I turn to look back the way I came and see him walk out of the shadows. He looks to his left and then to his right. His eyes zero in on me in the back of the cab. I see his shoulders fall, relief or disappointment washing over him, I'm not sure which. Probably relief. A guy like that doesn't get disappointed when a girl like me leaves without being asked.

I turn back around in my seat and face forward, thinking over what I have just done. I had my first one-night stand. I mean, he didn't take me back to his apartment, I didn't have to sneak out of bed, but that's not what makes it a one-night stand, is it?

For the sake of the list, I'm going to say no. I had sex with a complete stranger, and I have no intention of seeing him again. That is definitely a one-night stand.

WHEN I WAKE in the morning, I expect to feel a lot dirtier than I do. I never did the sleeping around thing because I thought sex wouldn't be as good with a random person, that I needed to connect with him on a deeper level. But that was not the case with…damn, I don't even know his name.

I push the thoughts away and go for a shower. I turn the water on to let it heat up as I begin to pull off my clothes. I happen to catch a glimpse of something in the mirror that makes me do a double take. I have fresh bruises on my hips that wrap around to my backside.

I laugh and cover my mouth as I inspect the mirror closer. When my hand falls back at my side, I see my bottom lip is slightly swollen and a bruise stains it as well. It's barely even visible, but I know it's there.

Just seeing the marks he left on my skin sends a rush through me. My stomach muscles tighten, wanting more of him. I roll my eyes and shake my head. That's never going to happen.

WHEN I GET out of the shower and dress for the day, I pick up my list and mark through, "Have a one-night stand" and "Dance in public."

Every time I mark something off this list, a smile forms as a blanket of comfort falls over me, warming me. It's like Katie is giving me a hug for achieving the small goal.

I toss the list to the side and grab my computer. I need to plan my trip to Miami to start her vacation. I know this is a completely crazy idea, but it's something I need to do for her. She never got to take the trip of a lifetime, as she called it, so I'm going to take it for her.

I look at the price of a plane ticket, but dread settles over me. Can I get on a plane? So soon after my best friend was killed on one? I could take a bus or train. Or maybe even rent a car and take a road trip. I pull up a car service and book a car, wanting to get on with her plans. I close the computer and grab my things. I have a list of my own to get done before taking this vacation.

I walk into the tanning salon I work at and stop at the counter. Jill, a girl I'm not too friendly with, is behind the counter making out with who I assume is a customer.

I knock on the glass counter. "Hello?"

They pull away from one another quickly.

"I'm so sorry," she starts, but then she sees that it's just me. "Oh, hey. What's up?" She straightens her too tight tank top, and brushes her disheveled bleach blonde hair away from her overly done face.

I smile sweetly, enjoying this entirely way too much. "I quit."

Her mouth falls open as her emerald eyes widen with surprise. "What? Why? You're supposed to relieve me this afternoon."

"Yeah… That's not going to happen. See ya!" I spin and walk out the door with a pep in my step. I laugh as I walk away. Jill wasn't expecting that at all. I've always been the reliable one, the one that was always called when someone couldn't come in. But I'm taking Katie's advice and quitting that dead-end job. I want no ties to this place or my old life.

It's time for a change.

I stop at a few stores and grab a new bikini, something I would never have chosen before. The top barely covers anything more than my nipples and the bottoms, if you can even call them that, are nothing more than a few strings put together. I also grab a new pair of sunglasses and flip flops.

Walking back to my apartment, the sun shines brightly down upon me, warming my skin. The warm breeze feels magical as it blows loose strands of hair around me. Quitting my job, I expected to feel panicked. I no longer have a steady income. But instead, I feel liberated. Finally free from a dead-end job that provided me nothing but a small income.

As I'm walking down the street, high on my most recent accomplishments, I see an Indian restaurant up ahead. I've always avoided it because it's known for its incredibly spicy food. My feet stop moving as I think it over. It's not that I'm afraid to eat spicy food, it's just that the pain outweighs the gain. But I guess not everything on this list will be fun for me. Some things are purely there just to make me uncomfortable, make me try different things to get me out of my element.

I take a deep breath and push on.

I walk the few steps into the restaurant and the smell of the spice lingers in the air. It burns my tongue and throat just from breathing.

"Table for one?" the hostess asks.

I nod. "Yes, please."

She leads me to a small two-person table and hands me a menu. Already I feel out of my element, and I haven't even had to order yet.

"What can I get you to drink?" she asks, standing up straight with her hands clasped at her waist.

God, I don't know. What will help with the burn? "Just water, please."

She bows her head before rushing off to get my water.

I start looking through the menu, not knowing what anything is. I look at the people around me to see what they are eating, but honestly, it all looks the same to me.

I feel defeated.

I feel my skin prickle and a tingling forms in my stomach. I begin looking around me, wondering why I'm feeling this way. I gaze around the room, twisting in my seat to see behind me. My eyes lock on familiar bright blue ones.

I turn around quickly. *Oh, fuck. This is not happening.* I rub my temples as my eyes flutter shut.

He saw me. I know he saw me. Please don't let him come over here. I pray that he accepts last night for what it was and doesn't make this awkward.

"I didn't think I'd get lucky enough to see you again."

Fuck. I should have known I couldn't get that lucky.

I look up at his ocean colored eyes and swallow down my fear. "I didn't either," I answer as I look him over. Yesterday he was dressed in a suit for the funeral, and when he showed up at the club, he hadn't bothered to change. But today, he looks completely different. Today, he's wearing a pair of jeans that hang slightly from his hips, a pair of black sneakers, and his black t-shirt hugs his hard chest and muscular arms. He looks younger and carefree. Hot as hell.

He nods toward the chair across from me. "Mind if I sit with you?"

My eyes flash around the busy restaurant, scrambling to come up with an excuse.

He sits down despite my lack of reply. "I can see that you're back to being your old worried self." His smug grin is back and it annoys me.

I roll my eyes. "You don't know anything about me."

One of his eyebrows raise as he shrugs. "I read people pretty well," he says, being completely abrasive.

I lean forward, challenging him. "Oh yeah? What do you see when you read me then?"

He leans back in his seat, confidence rolling off his

strong frame. "I'm afraid I will offend you." He rubs his angular jaw like he couldn't care less what we're talking about.

"Well then you don't read people as well as you think because I don't offend easily." I can't help the competitiveness he brings out in me.

"Yeah, okay," he says in a mocking tone with a roll of his eyes.

My mouth hangs open and my eyebrow arches. "You don't believe me?"

He shakes his head. "Not in the slightest."

I wet my lips and draw them into a tight line before adjusting my top and sitting up straight. "Try me. Hit me with your best shot."

His bright blue eyes darken with mischief as he leans forward. His grin still hasn't left his lips. It's like he knows he is about to wreck me. "Have it your way." He pops his neck like he's getting ready for a fight. "You're very closed off and shy. I think that you keep people at arm's length, and only let those closest to you know the real you. It's like you put on a show for the rest of the world, and it's so tiring that by the time you get home in the evenings, you can't even force yourself to socialize with another human being. I think last night was just the beginning of the new you. That you liked getting fucked against a dirty brick wall in an alley behind a club. And I think you got a whole lot more than what you were looking for last night." Each word he says is deep and husky, filled with a desire that only fuels my own.

I'm so caught up in what he's saying because he's dead on. "What do you think I was looking for, and what do you think I found?"

"I think you were looking for someone to help you forget for a moment."

"And that's exactly what I found, wasn't it?" I question.

He shakes his head. "You found more than that."

My face scrunches up on its own, not understanding what he's saying.

He picks up on my questions. "You found someone who's just as broken as you are. Someone who needs an escape… just like you."

I open my mouth to ask him what that's supposed to mean, but the waitress is back and placing my water in front of me.

"Are you ready to place your order?" she asks, politely.

"Oh!" I pick up my menu and attempt to look over it again. "I have no idea. I've never eaten here before."

There is a long list on the menu, and by each selection is a picture of a pepper. I look at the top of the menu and see they gauge the spiciness of the dish with the number of peppers on the side. I glance down until I find the first one with three peppers. I point at it and show her the menu. "I'll take that one."

She moves her palm against her chest. "Are you sure? That's a very brave order for someone who's never eaten here before."

I nod. "Yep, that's what I'll have."

She looks at the man sitting across from me. "I'll have the same," he tells her.

I hand my menu to the waitress before looking at him. "You don't even know what I ordered."

He shrugs. "I've had everything on their menu. It doesn't matter what it is."

I realize I still don't know his name and embarrassment settles over me because this man knows me in ways nobody else does.

"Well if you're going to crash my lunch, I think I need to know your name."

"Are you sure you want to know? That won't break the spell for you?" The corners of his lips turn up just a bit.

How does he know so much about me? Am I really that transparent? "Seeing you again today after what we did last night has already broken the spell," I lie. "So I think knowing your name is okay."

He lets out a small laugh. "It's River."

River...that's a weird name. "Don't you want to know mine?"

The waitress places a glass of water on the table in front of him and he picks it up, taking a drink. "I already know your name, Jovi."

"What? How do you know that?"

He lets out a deep laugh. "Calm down, I'm not stalking you if that's what you're thinking. I heard your dad tell George yesterday. That's how I knew you were outside."

Oh. That makes sense.

The waitress places our meal down in front of us and the smell of the food wafts up, stinging my eyes and making them water.

"What's the matter?" River asks, picking up his fork to eat.

"I don't like spicy food."

"Then why did you order the spiciest thing on the menu?"

I open my mouth to tell him *because of the list*,' but then think that maybe I shouldn't tell him about that. That list is between Katie and I. I don't want to share that secret with anyone else. Plus, he'd probably think I was completely crazy.

"It's just something I thought I needed to try." I shrug as I pick up my fork and poke at the sliver of meat.

He shakes his head, not understanding, as he takes a bite of his own food. "Do you want to order something else?"

I shake my head. "Nope. I ordered this, and I'm going to eat it." I raise the fork to my mouth and take a bite. The slice of chicken is already hot and burning my mouth so the spiciness of it doesn't even register…until I swallow. Then my mouth feels like it's on fire. My eyes start to water as my mouth stings.

I stick my tongue out and try fanning it with my hands. When that doesn't work, I grab my glass of water and chug down as much of it as I can. The burning on my tongue is what I imagine hell to feel like. If I didn't know any better, I'd think my mouth was melting.

River's laugh cuts through me, and I turn my angry gaze at him. "What's so funny? I'm in pain here!"

He throws his head back, laughing even harder.

I reach across the table and smack his shoulder. "What's wrong with you? Make it stop!" My eyes are completely filled with tears now. They are running down my face faster than I can wipe them away. But my tearstained face is not what I'm worrying about. I'm worried about never being able to taste anything ever again because I know my taste buds are burning off right now.

All my yelling at River and acting like a complete crazy person gets the attention of the waitress and she rushes over with a glass. "Drink this."

I take the glass, more than willing to drink anything that will put me out of my misery. I chug the magical substance, that just so happens to be milk, and little by little, the burning subsides. I set the empty glass on the table while she stands back watching with a look that says *I told you so*.

"Oh, that's so much better. Thank you."

She nods with her arms crossed over her chest and walks away.

I use my napkin to dry my face as I look back up at River. He's just sitting there eating like nothing is going on.

I feel my eyebrow raise. "Are you serious? How can you even eat that?"

He shrugs. "I like it."

"I hate spicy food." I toss my napkin down on the table

and scoot my chair back. "In fact, I think I'm going to go pay and get out of here." I stand without telling him goodbye and turn towards the register.

The waitress who waited on my table is now behind the counter. When I walk up, she smiles and waves me on.

"Are you sure? I don't want you to get in trouble."

She nods. "It happens all the time."

I can only imagine. "Thank you," I tell her with a kind, appreciative smile.

I push open the door and step out onto the sidewalk. I'm only a few steps away when River rushes out behind me.

"Hey!"

I stop and turn to face him. "You are a really bad stalker. You know, you're not supposed to let me see you."

He rolls his eyes. "I'm not stalking you. What are you doing today?"

I shrug as I begin walking again. "I have to pack."

"Pack?" he sounds alarmed as his feet stop moving.

"Yeah, I'm taking a trip," I say over my shoulder.

He jogs until he catches back up to me. "Where to?"

I look at him, feeling a smile tugging at my lips. "What's it to you?"

"I'm just making conversation, Jovi."

"I'm not the best at conversation," I say without slowing as I jog across the street.

He keeps pace with me, and once we're across the street, he grabs me by the crook of my arm, stopping me.

"Let's stop in here and grab a drink." He motions towards the small pub we're standing in front of.

My head cocks to the side while I look over at him, studying him. "Look, I didn't mean for you to fall in love with me or anything last night. That broken girl you met yesterday and saw last night, that's not me."

He rolls his eyes yet again. "Don't be so full of yourself." He grabs me by my shoulders and walks me in the door.

5

HE PRACTICALLY PUSHES ME UP TO THE BAR AND ONTO A barstool before motioning for the bartender.

I make myself comfortable, hanging my purse on the hook under the bar, as he orders us a drink.

He takes the seat next to me and I look over at him, trying to figure him out and what he wants with me.

"What are you staring at?" he asks, seeing me out of the corner of his bright blue eyes.

"I'm trying to figure out what your deal is."

He turns his body to face me. "Why do I have to have a 'deal'?"

I shrug as the bartender places our drinks in front of us. I pick up the glass and take a sip as he slides over some cash. "I don't know. We met under these really weird circumstances, and then we had a random hook up. I never expected to see you again."

He sets his drink down and trains his eyes on me. "Let me ask you this, why did you kiss me yesterday?"

I turn to look at myself in the mirror hanging behind the bar. I don't want him to see me, see that I'm lying. "As a thank you for the drink." The lie leaves my lips smoothly. I almost buy it myself.

"Bullshit. What's the real reason?"

I turn to him suddenly with my mouth hanging open from him calling me out. "It's none of your business."

He laughs. "It's none of my business why you felt the need to sexually assault me?" He leans back, amusement written all over his perfectly sculpted face. His eyes shine bright, even under the dim lights of the bar.

Now it's my turn to laugh. "Sexual assault? I don't think that's what it was." I pick up my drink and take another swig, enjoying the burn it brings and the numbness that accompanies it.

"Did I give you the impression that I wanted you to kiss me?"

I squint my eyes at him. What is he getting at? "No."

"Then why did you do it?" His eyes hold a gleam of wicked amusement. He likes challenging me.

I let out a deep breath. "A friend of mine made me this summer bucket list," I admit a little breathless.

He nods like he understands. "And this list said 'kiss

River'?" His voice is dead serious, but the expression on his face is nothing short of sarcastic.

"No. It said 'kiss a stranger'," I say, annoyance consuming me as I push my dark hair behind my ear.

He holds his arms up at his sides. "So why me? What made you decided that I was the stranger you should kiss?"

God he annoys me so much! "I don't know. You were there, the list popped into my head. I figured, why not? I had never seen you before in my life and I figured I never would again."

"Ahh, so you took this bucket list challenge, but you decided to play it the safe way."

"What do you mean the safe way?" I want to get up and leave because he pushes these buttons inside of me that make me want to pull my hair out. It's like he's a child that just lives to annoy me. But something inside of me won't let me walk away that easy. It's like I'm a glutton for punishment, and just have to see what he will say next.

He pulls his barstool a bit closer, causing his legs to be on either side of mine. Our legs are almost touching and it causes a tingle to take over. "Okay, this list, I'm assuming, was meant to get you out of your element, to make you do things you'd never do, and to learn to live with what comes out of it instead of always playing it safe, right?" His jaw flexes as he waits for the answer.

I nod. "Yeah, I guess."

"Well, you're not playing right."

A puff of air leaves me in a rush. "There are no rules!"

He holds up his finger. "That's where you're wrong. Why bother with the list if you're not going to do it right? You thought you could cross things off without having to deal with the consequences. Meaning, you kissed me because you thought you wouldn't have to mess with the awkwardness of having to run into me."

I bite the inside of my cheek while I think it over. But I can't come up with an argument because he's right. I'm not doing this right. I need to put myself out there and learn what it's like to be truly vulnerable.

I pick up my glass and finish it off.

River, apparently happy with the inner turmoil he's caused in me, leans back, smiling like a Cheshire cat. I want to reach over and smack that smug look right off his face.

After a good, long minute of silence, I turn to him. "So what should I do then? Just go up to a random stranger in here and kiss them?"

He looks around, surveying the small pub. "Yeah, go kiss that one." He nods towards the back corner.

I turn to look and see only a couple sitting over in the direction he'd indicated. The guy is looking around the bar, looking completely uninterested in his date, and the girl is leaning in close, talking his ear off.

I look back at River. "Um, they look like they are on a date."

His wicked smile comes back. "I know."

I smack his arm. "Are you trying to get me beat up?"

He scoffs. "She won't beat you up. She'd be too worried about breaking a nail. She might slap him though."

I turn to face the bartender, showing him my empty glass. "No way. I'm not doing that." I'm shaking my head vigorously.

He nudges me with his shoulder. "There you go playing it safe again."

I spin to him in anger. "What good could come out of doing that?"

"You would learn to be free, to take what you want. To fuck up, and deal with the consequences. To take a fucking risk, Jovi." He shakes his head like he's getting angry with me.

The bartender hands me another drink and I look at River to pay. He seems taken back.

"Hey, you dragged me in here. So to me, that means you're buying."

He sighs and hands over the money.

I throw my drink back and sit up straight, adjusting my shirt because suddenly, I feel very uncomfortable.

"You look fine. Just do it already."

I look over at him and he's smiling. But it's not the shit eating grin like usual, the one that is always excited to start trouble. This looks like one of true happiness. Is there a reason he wants me to kiss this guy, or is he just happy to get me to try something I never would?

"Fine." I stand and turn towards the couple. My stomach fills with butterflies as it rolls around with nerves.

The man's eyes meet mine and he watches me curiously, but also like he wants to eat me up.

I force myself to stop thinking about what I'm doing. I mean, what if this couple is married? I could be ruining a marriage. My eyes flash to their hands.

Nope, no rings.

I approach their table and he looks up at me. The woman he's with finally stops talking as her eyes land on me with a dirty look. I lean over, placing my hand at the base of his neck, and move my lips to his. He doesn't stop me. In fact, he seems to enjoy it because his hand flies up to tangle into my hair, holding me to him.

I break the kiss and look into his eyes. Before turning to leave, I bite his bottom lip, tugging, until I release it with a pop. He pulls his lip between his teeth as he watches me walk slowly away.

I feel completely fucking exhilarated. "I can't believe I did that!" I practically squeal as I get closer to River who's been sitting in place, watching everything unfold.

He stands to celebrate with me and I leap into his arms, hugging him close. His arms wrap around me and our eyes meet. Something is happening. We're exchanging something, but I have no idea what it is.

Suddenly, something breaks and he averts his eyes to the corner. "We should probably go." He lets out a laugh before grabbing my purse and pushing me towards the door.

Before I step out, I hear a high pitched, "who was that, you jerk?"

We both step outside, laughing. I laugh so hard I'm holding my stomach as tears stream down my overheated cheeks.

"Did you see her face?" River asks, wiping the tears away from his eyes as we walk down the street.

I nod as my laughter dies down. We're stopped, waiting for the crosswalk sign to light up. I turn to see his eyes radiating happiness. They lock on mine as he wets his lips with his tongue. His teeth scrape against his bottom lip, and before I know what's happening, he's pulling me flush against him in a lip crushing kiss.

His lips are hot against mine and his tongue tastes like a mixture of liquor and his own sweet flavor. His right hand is cupping my cheek while the other is on my hip, holding me to him.

My stomach muscles tighten and my nipples poke against my shirt with confusion and excitement pumping through me.

With his lips on mine, I'm reminded of the previous night when he completely fucking owned me against that wall, and instantly, I want him again despite how much he bothers me.

I break the kiss and look up at him. His eyes have darkened again, and his lips are wet from our kiss.

"Why are you looking at me like that, princess?" His voice is deep and husky. Sexy.

I bite my lower lip and avert my eyes, suddenly feeling nervous.

"Just tell me what you want and it's yours," he says, pushing a strand of hair behind my ear.

I feel my face heat up as I look back up at him. "I want you to make me feel again."

He cocks his head slightly to the side and his jaw flexes. "Where do you live?"

I UNLOCK the door and the second it's open, he spins me around, picking me up in his strong, muscular arms.

He walks us into my apartment and kicks the door shut with his foot while he presses me against the wall, lips moving quickly with mine. My hands thread through his blond hair as his lips slide down my neck. His teeth nip my sensitive skin, and a breathy moan leaves me.

His hands tug at my shirt until I allow him to pull it from my body. Our hands and lips are all over, wanting to explore every inch of each other.

When his fingers unclasp my bra and it falls from my body, my face flushes. He never completely saw me the other night. We'd kept all our clothes on out in the open. But now, in the middle of the day, in my bright, white apartment with the sun openly streaming in through the windows, he's going to see everything.

He picks up on my sudden shyness, and he leans away. "You're fucking perfect." His lips find my jaw before they trail down my neck. He falls to his knees before sucking my hard nipple into his mouth, taking away any doubt I had. I can't think of anything else when he's touching me, teasing me.

His hands are massaging my breasts, and his tongue keeps dancing around my hard nipple. My entire body is tense as a storm brews inside of me. Without his mouth leaving me, his hands fall to unbutton my jeans. He sits back on his knees and pushes them down my legs, fully taking me in.

My eyes were locked on his, but standing in front of him completely bare with everything stripped away but my insecurities, my eyes close, not being able to watch him as he looks over my body.

I feel his hand softly run up my thigh before his lips press against my stomach, causing every muscle to tense with fear and excitement. Finally, I look down at him.

His eyes are smoldering, and his jaw is flexed as he stands up in front of me. "You're not getting all shy on me now, are you?" He leans in, nipping my bottom lip.

"This is different for me." I can hear the nerves dripping from my words. "I don't usually stand here and let a man study my naked body."

The corner of his mouth turns up into a lopsided grin. "I'm not studying. I'm admiring. You're fucking sexy, and I'm going to fucking enjoy watching you crumble in my hands."

His lips crash into mine as his finger slides into me

without warning. He pulls it out to spread my wetness around my aching sex before dipping back inside.

I lace my fingers into his hair and slightly pull, causing him to groan against my lips as he kisses me even harder.

He removes his fingers from me and cups my ass with both hands before picking me up and walking us through my apartment. He finds my bedroom, and he drops me on the bed. I lie flat, watching as he pulls off his shirt, revealing his hard, muscular chest and biceps.

God, how did I not know he was hiding all that?

I lick my lips, in desperate need to taste his gorgeous body.

"What is it, princess?" he asks, looming over me with the darkness of desire dancing in his eyes. He unbuttons his jeans and ever so fucking slowly, slides them down his muscular thighs. His large cock stands to attention, and my eyes are drawn to it.

"I want to taste you," I nearly whisper as I get up on all fours to move to the foot of the bed.

He steps closer and I moisten my lips, opening for him. His velvety soft tip slides against my tongue, and I swirl it around him. His hands tangle in my hair as his breathing picks up. I take him as far as I can go before sliding him back out. When my lips are on his tip, I look up and see his eyes have closed and his mouth is agape.

I've only slid him in and out of my mouth a few times, but I can taste his arousal dripping from his tip. Suddenly, he pulls my hair until I release him. He places his finger under my chin, directing me to sit up on my knees. I do as he wants, putting my forehead at his lips. "My turn to taste you," he says against my skin.

His lips find mine as he crawls onto the bed, urging me backward until I'm lying on my back again. When he breaks the kiss, he's eye level with me as he holds himself off me. "Did I do this to you?" His voice is almost pained as his hand softly touches my hip.

"I didn't notice it until this morning."

He lowers himself to my hips, showering the bruises with kisses. "I'm sorry. I didn't realize how rough I was being."

I smile shyly at him, almost embarrassed to admit how much I enjoyed what we did. "I enjoyed every minute of last night, but I think you already knew that."

"Let me make you forget all about last night." His hands grab hold of my hips, rolling us over as he directs me to hover above his face. While his tongue laps me, his hands squeeze my ass.

My hands are flat against the wall in front of me, supporting myself so I don't fall while he works me over. His tongue is hot and soft, but forceful as it flicks against my sensitive nub. Every muscle in my body is practically singing, aching for my release. As it slowly builds, he slides his fingers into me, stoking that spot that has me quivering with need.

My eyes close automatically as the waves of my orgasm wash over me stronger than ever. I've had sex several times, but no man has ever done this or made me feel this way.

I can feel myself convulsing around him and it only makes him move quicker. By the time my orgasm ends, my skin is covered in a sheen of sweat with my hair clinging to my sticky neck and back.

"Are you ready for me?" he asks as he slides out from under me.

The words don't have time to leave my lips before he's thrusting into me, filling me from behind. I clench the pillows with both hands as he slides into me, rolling his hips before pulling back out. I try to see him over my shoulder, but my hair is covering my eyes, and I don't dare to move it out of the way. I feel like if I don't hold on to something, I will fall right off the edge of the earth.

He pumps into me hard and fast. The sounds of our heavy breathing and our skin slapping together fills the room. We're both completely drenched in sweat. It beads up and drips from his chin, landing on my lower back.

His hand fists in my hair, tugging my head back and to the side where our lips meet. I suck the taste of me off his tongue. This only makes him double his efforts until we're both panting and screaming with our release.

I WAKE SOMETIME LATER and the room is dark. The full wall of windows across from my bed is still uncovered, showing the dark clouds that loom nearby. I sit up and look around me, but River is gone.

I let out a quick chuckle. Serves me right for doing the same thing to him last night.

I stand from the bed and walk across the floor completely naked, into my bathroom to shower. I take my time, washing every inch of myself slowly while thinking over the best sex I've ever had in my life.

Nick, my ex-boyfriend, he never did the things that River has done to me. With Nick, it was more like a race to get off. But with River, it's like the ride is half the fun. His release isn't the important part for him. He likes to see how much he can turn me on before ever sliding into me.

A warmth spreads through my body when I think about him, and that scares me. I shouldn't be having these feelings about him. I don't know him, and something tells me River isn't the relationship type. The relationship type doesn't pick up a random girl in a club and fuck her in the back alley.

I'm just a fun-pass for him. And you know what, I'm okay with that. I don't need to complicate things with a relationship right now. I don't need these lingering feelings that happen after we have sex either. I need to learn to let things go, to have fun in the moment, and accept when it ends.

I dry myself off before pulling on an oversized t-shirt. I towel-dry my hair, but don't bother brushing it.

All the strenuous activity I've done today has my

stomach growling. I head towards the kitchen to find something for dinner.

6

I'M PULLING MY WET HAIR UP INTO A BUN AS I WALK DOWN the hallway. I round the corner and head for the fridge.

"Hey."

I scream and clutch at my chest. "What the fuck? You scared the shit out of me," I yell at River while trying to calm my pounding heart.

He laughs. "Sorry." He places a pan he pulled out of the oven onto the stovetop. "I figured I'd cook some dinner."

I grab a bottle of water out of the fridge and sit at the island. "You're cooking me dinner?"

He shrugs while moving about, gathering things he needs. "I'm cooking us dinner."

I take a sip and place the cap back on the bottle. "I thought you had left."

He stops buttering the rolls and looks up at me through his thick eyelashes. "What kind of person sneaks out of bed and leaves without warning?"

I shrug. "Maybe the same kind of person who runs away as soon as the other turns their back to dress."

He points the butter knife in my direction. "I'll let that one slide. You didn't know I was the man of your dreams then." His cocky grin makes me laugh and shake my head.

"So, what are you making?" I ask to change the subject. The food smells wonderful and I can't help but feel hungry.

He places the rolls into the bread basket and covers them with a cloth napkin. "I made chicken parmesan."

"Really? That sounds fancy." I stand and pull down two plates from the cabinet and hand each of them to him to serve the food.

"It's nothing. I couldn't make much. Do you ever go shopping?"

"Not unless I have to. I usually order pizza or Chinese." I take the plates and carry them over to the table. He follows behind me with the basket of rolls.

We sit down, and I cut into my chicken and take a bite. "Wow! This is great. Where'd you learn to cook like this?"

"My mom for the most part. And just living on my own and having to figure things out."

"I've lived on my own for four years now and I still haven't figured out how to cook."

He smiles and it makes my heart flutter. "So this trip, where are you going?"

My eyes fall to my plate. I don't like talking about Katie. It makes a spot deep inside me hurt. "Um, to Miami," I finally answer.

"When do you leave?" he asks, not looking up at me.

"I reserved a car for tomorrow."

He sets his fork and knife down and glares at me, completely unmoving. "You mean you plan on driving across the country by yourself?" His voice is full of alarm.

I scoff. "Yeah. Why not?"

"I'm coming with you," he says, jaw twitching and eyes growing darker by the second.

My fork clatters to my plate. "What?"

"There's no fucking way you're driving across the country alone. What are you even thinking?"

"I'm thinking that I need to take this trip and getting on a plane isn't an option right now." I can feel the anger leaving my body in thick waves. I'm sure he can feel it too because it's all directed at him.

The anger lines between his eyes are starting to smooth out, like he understands the underlined meaning there. "Why isn't a plane an option?"

I squint my eyes at him, slightly incredulous. "You know why."

He blinks and slowly nods his head, understanding. "I get it, I do. But do you know how dangerous driving across the country is? You'll be stopping at truck stops all alone for gas. You'll be staying in shady motels by yourself."

"I don't even know *you*!"

He rolls his blue eyes. "So it's okay for you to sleep with someone you don't know, but you can't take a trip with me?"

A laugh escapes me. "I don't know." I shake my head and rub my temples. "This is all fucked up. You were meant to be a one-time thing." I stand and place my plate in the sink before turning to lean against the counter, no longer hungry.

He stands and his gaze locks on mine. "It's all about trying something new and dealing with the consequences, remember?"

I'm holding onto the counter behind me for dear life as my breathing picks up. I don't know why, but suddenly, I'm nervous. It may be the way his blue eyes darken with this intense conversation. It may be the way his jaw is cocked or the bobbing of his Adam's apple. Or, it could be the way he's slowly closing in on me.

Why is he doing this to me? He was supposed to be a one-time thing. I've never expected him to keep showing up, and I certainly never expected to want him this much.

He finally closes the distance between us as he comes to a stop directly in front of me. He places his palms flat against the counter behind me so he's slightly leaning over me, but he's not touching me even though we're practically nose to nose.

"Can I join you on your trip?" His breath blows across my face, making me wet my dry lips.

"No," I answer, still overwhelmed with anger.

He runs his tongue across his thick bottom lip as he moves in, lips almost touching. "Can I join you on your trip?"

I look into his dark eyes, and with our mouthes almost touching, I feel myself caving. It would be nice to not be alone on this trip, despite how much he annoys me. "On one condition."

"What's that?" he whispers, eyes still locked on mine.

I stand up straight, causing him to do the same. "You have to help me cross off this list. It has to be done by the end of summer."

He grins. "That I can do."

WE MEET up at the car rental bright and early the next morning, each with our bags.

"Are you ready?" I ask him.

"You got the list?"

I nod and smile before tossing my bag into the trunk.

I get behind the wheel and start the car while he takes the seat next to me. As I'm pulling out of the parking lot, he asks, "so where is this list?"

I reach into my purse between us and pull out the notebook, handing it over to him. He leans back in his seat, reading over every item.

It's quiet for a long time while I follow along the route I mapped out. Finally, he tosses the notebook on top of my purse. "I think we can get all this done by the end of the summer."

"Really?" I look over at him with a big smile.

He nods. "Yeah, I mean, some are simple, everyday things. How have you made it this far without doing a keg stand?"

I laugh out loud. "Katie and I went to a party once, and she was determined to get me to do one. She never managed it though. Leave it to her to pull it over on me now."

He grows silent as he turns his eyes back to the road. "Katie made this list?"

I didn't even mean to talk about her. It was such a fun memory, it just slipped out when he mentioned it. A shadow of sadness falls over me. "Yeah."

"Why are you taking this trip? Wasn't Katie's plane heading toward Miami when it crashed?"

His question makes my blood run cold. I tighten my grip on the steering wheel. I wasn't prepared to talk about her, about any of this. God, if I had only kept my mouth shut.

I nod, not able to find my voice.

"What is it you hope to achieve by taking this trip?" He's not being an asshole, he genuinely sounds interested. Like maybe he's afraid it will fall short for me and he doesn't want me to be let down.

I suck my bottom lip into my mouth and bite it while thinking it over. I want to answer his question, but I don't want to give away too much to make him ask more. Talking about Katie, it's not something I'm ready to do yet. Every time I hear her name, a pain slices through me. The wound is still too fresh, and talking about her is like pouring acid over that wound.

He's staring at me, waiting for my answer so I take a deep breath. "She asked me to go on that trip with her, but I said no. I couldn't afford it, and I didn't want her paying my way. And then after…" I hope he knows what I mean by *after* because I can't mention the crash or her death. "I found a letter from her. She wanted me to join her."

"You're not hoping to get there and have some sort of sign or spiritual connection, are you?"

I look over at him and see how worried he is.

I laugh. "No, that's insane. I'm just taking the trip she never got to. I have to live for the both of us now." I pull the necklace George gave me with her ashes, out from under the collar of my shirt. "She's taking this trip with me."

His eyes flicker down to the charm in my hand and his eyes glaze over with sadness before he turns his head back to the road. "What is that?"

"It's her ashes. Well, some of her ashes. George gave it to me that day at his house."

He nods but lines form around his eyes.

"Are you mad about something?"

"No, why would you think that?" he asks, still not looking at me.

I shrug. "You just seem mad. How did you know Katie anyway?"

"I'm just a friend of the family… more like an acquaintance actually."

"Did you ever meet her?" I turn to study him.

He looks at me and answers, "yeah, several times."

"And?" I feel my brows raise with the question.

"And what?"

I take a deep breath, hoping to gain a little bit of confidence. "Were you in love with her?" I ask because I couldn't stand sleeping with a guy that is in love with my best friend. It would feel like I am some kind of sad replacement or something.

"No!" His voice raises as he shakes his head at me.

I laugh out loud. "Okay, sorry for asking."

He crosses his arms over his chest and leans back, watching the road from beneath his lashes as our conversation comes to a screeching halt.

I DRIVE for most of the day, not stopping until the sun starts to set. We decide to find a cheap motel and some dinner and start back on our way tomorrow.

We've only just made it into Arizona, but already, I feel like I've been trapped in that car for days.

We find a small town with one gas station, a diner, and a motel. The town practically looks deserted. The pavement is sunbaked, like it hasn't been maintained in a long time, and weeds are growing up on the shoulders of the road. Wild flowers fill up the large ditches, and I can smell nothing but the hot tar of the pavement, and manure like maybe a farm is nearby.

The only good thing about this place is that all three of the businesses form a triangle. No need to go running through town to find anything. We have everything we need right here to stay the night and pick back up tomorrow.

We leave our bags in the trunk while we walk across the street to get some dinner. When we open the door, the bell rings and all four customers inside look directly at us.

"Not much goes on in this town, I can see," River whispers in my ear.

I smile and dig my elbow into his ribs, but drag him to a table in the corner, hoping everyone forgets we're here.

The young waitress greets us and sets down two menus. "Can I start you off with something to drink?"

"Yes, I'll have an iced tea," I reply while looking over my menu.

I look up to see the look she's giving River, and instantly I'm jealous. Doesn't she see me sitting here? For all she knows, we could be a couple.

She smiles and she bats her obnoxiously fake eyelashes at him. My teeth grind together absentmindedly.

I don't hear what he tells her over my thoughts, but when she walks away, his laughter cuts through me.

My eyes snap up to his. "What are you laughing at?"

"Could you look any more jealous?"

I scoff. "I'm not jealous."

"Oh, really?" His eyebrows rise with the question.

"Really," I state matter-of-factly.

"So you wouldn't care if I asked her out after her shift then?" He's not looking at me any longer, he's looking after the dark haired waitress whose uniform is entirely way too tight.

I feel my eyes grow wide with alarm, but reign in my jealously. "Be my guest. I have no claim to you."

His amused expression is gone, replaced with the flexing of his jaw and flaring of his nostrils. He picks up his menu and looks it over.

The waitress is back and she looks at River for his order.

"I'll just take a double bacon cheeseburger and fries," he tells her, handing over the menu.

She turns to me for my order, but she's still watching him out of the corner of her gray eyes.

"I'll have a cheeseburger with no mustard and fries."

She writes something down, and takes my menu before turning and walking away, shaking her ass more than needed.

I lean back in the booth and sip my tea, stirring it so the ice clinks off the glass.

"So you really think you have no claim to me?" River breaks the silence.

"Do you think I should? I mean, we met, what? Two days ago."

He leans back, acting like he doesn't care about anything going on around him. His eyes travel from mine, down my neck, and to my chest. "I bet your body thinks differently." He offers up a smug grin.

My flesh breaks out in goosebumps from the way he's looking at me. His dark eyes are practically lighting my insides on fire.

I laugh as my face heats up. "You really are full of yourself, aren't you?"

He looks around the restaurant. "Why wouldn't I be when all I have to do is look at you and your skin flushes? You still think I can't read you, but I know everything you're thinking right now, like how much you're wishing I was moving inside you, causing you to shatter around me." His voice is deep and rough, and the flexing of his jaw and the intensity of his dark eyes make me squeeze my thighs together, as desire reigns through my body.

His words turn me on, but I have to ignore that. I can't let him be right. I have to control myself.

I roll my eyes. "Okay, let's get one thing straight here." I tap my index finger on the table. "You are not God's gift to women. The way you affect me, is none of your concern. And you know what? It really doesn't say much about you anyway since I've only had sex during meaningful relationships. Did you ever think that maybe the reason I enjoy it as much as I do isn't because of you, but the thrill of not really knowing you? But rest assured, all of that will be gone by the end of this trip."

I expected to piss him off. I want to piss him off as much as he's pissing me off, but he smiles like he knows he's getting to me and it creates an irrational rage inside me. "Keep telling yourself that, sweetheart."

Really? That's it? I just went off on a rant like a crazy person and that's all he has to say? "God, you're so fucking annoying!"

He smiles wide and laughs before running his hand over the five o'clock shadow he's now sporting. It only makes him sexier, and I hate myself for even thinking that.

His laughing stops as the waitress places our plates in front of us. She practically throws mine down in front of me, but his, she places softly with a smile and doe eyes.

I snort. She may as well sit down and feed him too.

My snort draws both their eyes in my direction. River looks amused, but the waitress, not so much.

"Can I get you anything else?" she asks River sweetly.

He gives her a small smile and shakes his head with a polite no thanks.

When she walks away, he places his elbows on the table and sits up straight. "Would you like to try that again?" His blue eyes cut through me. They are getting darker by the second.

"Try what again?" I ask, my voice leaking nervousness from the way his eyes are taking me in and darkening with their journey.

"Trying to convince yourself that you have no claim to me."

"Whatever," is my great reply.

I'm not ready to admit anything yet. I can't be having feelings for him of all people. I mean, yes, he's sexy as fuck and knows how to manipulate my body like no one ever has, but he also annoys the shit out of me.

I pick up my burger and take a bite, immediately regretting it. I grab a napkin and spit the bite into it.

"What's wrong?"

I toss the napkin I just spit into down on the table. "It has mustard on it." My eyes automatically look around for the waitress who didn't get my order right because she was too busy checking out my— River.

"That's great!" His sexy smile makes me forget about my food while my stomach does flips.

I shake the tingles from my body. "How is that great? I'm hungry!"

"Number forty-seven on the list says, 'send back food'."

"Oh, no." I shake my head. "I can't do that one right now."

"What? Why?" His eyes narrow on me as his forehead wrinkles.

"Did you happen to see the looks that waitress was giving me? She will spit in it."

This has always been my fear. I mean, damn, I saw that movie about the food service workers. I haven't sent food back since, and I always get an uneasy feeling in my stomach when I think about how many times I had sent food back and just how much spit I must have consumed over the years.

"That's just part of dealing with the repercussions, remember?"

I look nervously around the outdated restaurant, a knot forms in my stomach.

"What do you have to lose? I mean, you won't eat it now anyway? You can at least cross it off the list."

I twist my fingers together in my lap. I guess he's right. I can at least eat my fries that are probably cold now.

"Okay." I take a deep breath and raise my hand.

River bursts out laughing. "What are you doing? You're not trying to answer a question in grade school." He grabs my arm and lowers it.

I shrug. "I don't know how to do this."

He spots our waitress and waves her over. She comes to a stop at our table with a beaming smile, until he motions towards me.

Her smile instantly drops as she turns her whole body to look at me.

I look at River and he nods me on. I swallow the excess slobber that's now pooling in my mouth at an alarming rate. "I ordered this with no mustard and there is mustard on it."

She rolls her eyes and lets out a dramatic sigh. "I'll have them make you a new one." She walks away without saying another word.

I feel my smile form on its own.

"See that wasn't so hard, was it?"

I shrug. "I guess not. But I'm still not eating it."

He quirks an eyebrow at me. "You have to eat at least one bite."

"Who made you the list police?" I grab a fry and bite it angrily.

He holds up his hands, silently agreeing not to mess with me.

7

Getting to Know one another

We walk across the street and pay for one night in the motel. I don't know where all my luck has gone, because out of this whole motel in this tiny, little town, the only room available had only one double bed. That means we both have to sleep in the same bed. I keep reminding myself that we have had sex twice now, but sleeping together, actually sleeping together feels too intimate.

River grabs both our bags out of the trunk while I unlock the door with an old school key. I open the door and flick on the light, the room fills up with a soft glow. But I'd rather have it dark so I didn't have to see the dirty, outdated room.

I feel my shoulders fall as River comes up behind me. "It's not bad," he says as he steps past me, dropping our bags on the floor and plopping down on the bed, the rusted, metal springs squeaking under his weight.

I feel my nose crinkle up.

He reads my expression. "It's only one night. It can't be *that* bad."

"Do you live in a barn or something? This room is horrible." I sit down in the chair in the corner.

I look around at the flattened brown carpet that is covered in stains. My eyes drift up to the old TV with bunny ears in front of the green, quilt covered bed. There are small wall lights that hang on either side of the bed, and two ratty old night stands.

"No, I live in the city, in a studio apartment."

"You really don't think this room is that bad?"

He purses his lips together and shakes his head. "Na, what's so bad about it? It has a bed to sleep in, a TV to watch, and a bathroom."

Oh, God. The bathroom. I didn't even think of that. I jump up and walk around the bed to the bathroom door. With a surge of bravery, I push the door open and flip the switch. A bright light fills the small space as my eyes adjust.

It's just as outdated as the rest of the room, but at least it's clean. The tiled walls are multiple shades of brown, and the handles on the old pedestal sink are rusted, but I don't see any used condoms or body hair attacking every surface. I let out a sigh of relief as I walk back into the room.

I stand at River's side. "Stand up."

He looks up at me with confusion written on his face. "Why?" he asks, but stands anyway.

I reach down and pull back the quilt, examining the sheets for any stains. No way can I sleep on someone else's bodily fluids. The sheets are crisp and white, free of any marks or holes.

"Do you feel better now?" he asks. I can hear the smirk I know is on his face.

I turn to look at him. "You may sit back down now."

He flops back onto the bed while I grab my bag and rifle through it. I grab some fresh clothes and spin around. "I'm taking a shower."

I turn on the shower and step under the stream of hot water. My back is sore from sitting in the car all day, and the heat of the water helps to soothe it. I rub my neck, trying to work out the knots.

Once I'm convinced the knots in my muscles are just a permanent part of me now, I use the shampoo provided and lather up my hair.

I'm just about to step out when I feel a cool gust of wind blow behind me. I twist around to see River.

"What the fuck are you doing?" I try hiding all my girlie bits.

His eyes go wide with alarm. "What? I need a shower too."

I push against his chest as I step out and wrap a towel around me. "We," I motion between us, "are not a couple!" I hold my towel tight around me. "Couples take showers together. We just…" I hold my hand up at my side and let it fall, it slaps off my thigh. "We just have sex on occasion and annoy one another."

He holds the shower curtain open, not ashamed of the full frontal view he's giving me as he grins, *fucking grins.* He shrugs one shoulder. "I thought this could be one of those occasions you speak of."

I practically growl as I grab my clothes and leave the bathroom. Stepping into the other room, I dress quickly and rake a brush through my dark hair, seething. How dare he even think he can get in the shower with me? In what world is it okay to just jump in the shower with someone when you're not invited?

Maybe I'm giving him mixed signals. But I don't mean to. Yes, I kissed him first, and yes, I guess I was the one to initiate sex, but that was supposed to be a random, one-time thing. Then, when he showed up and I kissed that guy in the bar, I was so high off my excitement and our kiss on the street corner, I threw caution to the wind. I never should have slept with him a second time. But my body wants him more than anything. I couldn't help the jealously when it came to that waitress. God, what is wrong with me? I cannot be falling for this guy.

I should keep my distance. I won't allow myself to think of his rock hard body, the way he can manipulate mine, or the earth shattering orgasms I've had at his hands. From now on, he's just a friend. A friend I'm not attracted to at all. That's all it is anyway: attraction. I'm not in love with him. He drives me completely fucking crazy.

I slide into bed and watch the black and white movie playing on the TV, but I'm not really watching it. I'm thinking about what I have gotten myself into.

Remembering to text my mom, I type out a quick message, telling her where I am and that I'm safe for the night before turning my phone off and dropping it onto the table. I settle back into bed.

The bathroom door suddenly opens and he walks into the room in his white boxer briefs. His strong chest is still slightly damp and it glistens with the soft glow of the room. As he passes in front of the TV, his whole body is fully visible, and my eyes skim down his six pack to that V that points right to his dick. I have no idea what that part of the body is called, but fuck my life, it does things to me it shouldn't.

Feeling extra irritated with myself, I roll my eyes as he walks closer to me. He struts his shit like a damn runway model, demanding my attention. He slides into bed next to me and the smell of his body-wash and shampoo sends a tingling fire from my stomach to directly between my legs.

"God, don't you have clothes?"

He turns to give me his cocky grin. "What's the matter, princess? Are you afraid you won't be able to keep your hands off me?"

I scoff. "Hardly."

"Well then my nearly naked appearance shouldn't bother

you." He raises his arms, placing them behind his head, elevating him enough to watch TV.

His scent washes over me again, strong and powerful. I breathe it in deeply, letting it take me back to that first night in the alley. I think about the way he held me firmly in his hands, the way he'd drilled into me hard and forceful, his cocky grin that pisses me off and turns me on at the same time, and I can feel the wetness pooling between my thighs.

I keep my eyes on the TV, refusing to do anything about my urges. There is seriously something wrong with me. I've never wanted a guy this much. Even the guys I dated before didn't have this much control over me with something as simple as their presence.

My heart pounds wildly in my ears and my flesh becomes sticky as my blood pressure rises, but I don't dare look at him.

I let out a long breath. "I need a drink." I cover my eyes with my forearm.

"Lucky for you I don't go anywhere without my flask." He stands and reaches into his bag. He pulls out the shiny metal flask and uncaps it. He takes a drink before handing it over. As I'm lying on my side, I prop my head up with my hand and take a drink. The warm alcohol pours into my mouth, burning its way down. It sets in my belly, warming it even more.

In an attempt to talk to keep my mind off what his body is doing to mine, I say, "I know nothing about you. Where are you from? Where do you work?"

He takes the flask and takes a sip. "I'm from New York. I just moved to the city about a month ago. In New York, I was in advertising, but I hated it. It was suffocating."

"What do you mean?"

He looks at me and thinks it over for a minute. "Did you ever hear the saying, leave your work at work?"

"Of course."

"That wasn't possible with advertising. It was all I thought about. All day at work we would create ads and try to figure out how to market whatever product we were working on. But when I was off work, all I saw was advertising. Most people tend to overlook the billboards, the posters plastered all over the walls of the subway, the advertisements on the sides of buses, but I couldn't. When I saw an ad, I wondered who created it, what made them think up that concept, how I could make it better. It was exhausting."

"I can honestly say that I've never given it much thought."

"Exactly. I worked myself to the bone and for what? So people like you could totally overlook all my hard work."

"I'm sorry," I begin, but he cuts me off.

"No. I didn't mean it like that. It was all just too impersonal. Everyone was doing the same things. It was like one person would come up with a good concept, and when everyone saw how well it was working, they would copy it. It just wasn't worth the annoyance anymore."

"So what? You just packed your bags and moved to California?"

He nods. "Basically. I wanted to get out of New York. I wanted to find myself, I guess."

"And have you found yourself?" I look up to meet his dark eyes.

"I'm starting to." His face is serious, but he has an easiness about him.

"How old are you, River?"

"Twenty-five," he answers.

"I'm only twenty-three, and I think you're already doing way better than I am. I haven't even had a career yet."

He looks deep into my eyes, causing my heart to jump up to my throat. "Why not? What did you go to college for?"

I take the flask from his hand and take another sip as I shrug. "I don't know. I just don't know what I want to do. I was the same way when I graduated high school, so I never went to college. What are you planning on doing since you're giving up advertising?"

He thinks it over for a quick second. "I don't know. I didn't have a plan when I moved here. I just want to find something that I love to do, something that won't slowly steal pieces of my soul."

Our eyes are locked together and my lips part with my heavy breathing. He looks down at my mouth before wetting his lips. Slowly, he leans in, pressing his soft, hot mouth to mine.

With the closeness of our conversation, I can't deny him what he's demanding. I simply can't. I don't know why, but despite all my earlier reserve, I want to give him all of me.

I tangle my fingers into his wet, blond hair and pull it gently while his lips and tongue move with mine. He rolls towards me, placing his hand on my jaw, his long fingers wrapping around the back of my neck as he holds me to him.

A soft whimper escapes me. He's moving so slow and cautiously, I can't keep it in. I feel him harden against my outer thigh, and my muscles tense with anticipation.

Without breaking the kiss, he places himself between my parted legs, pressing right where I need him to. His hand snakes up under my shirt, and he palms my breast while teasing my taut nipple.

The way his body feels against mine is nothing short of euphoric. He knows all the right places to touch to have me busting at the seams. Every inch of my skin craves this man: his touch, his taste, *him*.

He grinds against me in a rhythm that has me wanting to push him off so I can slide down his hard length. I'm dripping with need, and I haven't even lost an article of clothing yet. Our limbs are tangled together as our hands rush around one another's bodies unabashedly. I'm no longer trying to convince myself I don't want him. I'm trying to remember why I didn't want him in the first place because right now, he's all I want. He's strong and hard, and the way he's kissing me has me seeing stars.

His hands slide my sweat pants and panties down my

legs, and my shirt has long ago been pushed up to reveal my breasts. While his hands and mouth work me over, he continues to grind against me. I can feel my wetness soaking his boxers.

"You're always so fucking wet for me," he nearly growls as he strips his now wet underwear off his hips.

His lips crash with mine again, and with nothing between us, his thick cock presses right where it needs to. With one roll of his hips, he could be deep inside me. I waggle myself against him eagerly, hoping he enters me, even if it's just a little. I need relief from this pressure that's building up inside of me.

"Do you want me inside you, princess?" His voice is thick and rough, filled with need and determination.

"Yes," I practically pant out.

He's holding himself up by his elbows on either side of me as he looks down with his cocky grin. "Say it. I want to hear how badly you want me inside of you." His lips find my neck where he kisses and nibbles on the sensitive skin, further teasing me. His hard cock slides between my slick folds, causing a jolt of passion to run through me. Just when I think he's going to push inside me, he pulls away, only to repeat the process again.

"I want you inside of me. Now!"

He pulls his lips away from my neck. "That's all you had to say, sweetheart." Without regard, he thrusts into me deeply, making me call out and dig my nails into the skin of his back. He pulls out before sliding back in with powerful thrusts that push me up the bed. He's so big and hard, he completely fills every inch of me. The sudden fullness hurts, but in an absolutely pleasurable way.

His hands grip my hips, holding me so he can thrust even deeper. My eyes open to see his sculpted muscles flexing and moving while he owns me in every way possible. Our breathing is loud and erratic while our bodies get what they want. My toes go numb as my release builds higher and higher until I break around him.

When I come down from my high, he pulls out of me and turns me over, grabbing me by my hips and lifting me onto all fours. "I hope you didn't think I was done with you yet," he growls, sliding back into me. It feels like he's even bigger and going deeper in this position. I grasp the pillows firmly as the sound of our skin slapping and the bed squeaking fills the room.

The headboard begins banging off the wall every time he pushes back into me. I tighten myself around him, preparing to be ripped apart with another orgasm when he says, "touch yourself. I'm going to come and I can't stop it. Finish with me."

His movements never slow as I reach between my legs and circle the hard nub that surges with pleasure with every little touch. Every muscle in my body tenses even harder with my hand rubbing over my sensitive sex and him filling me. We both let out a moan of pleasure as our orgasms rush over us. I'm convulsing around him, milking him for every last drop.

He thrusts forward with a final shudder, before we both collapse, tangled together.

All I can hear is my heart pounding away like a jackhammer. My lungs burn, needing more oxygen, but I can't seem to get enough. Sweat clings to my body like a second skin as we lie together in the mess of sheets.

He rolls to his side to look at me, placing his hand on my jaw again. "Stop denying that you have no claim to me and just fucking admit you want me as badly as I want you. It's nothing to be ashamed of." He stands and walks to the bathroom, leaving me looking after him, wondering if he's right.

Should I just give up on trying to keep some distance between us? It seemed like an impossible task anyway. Maybe I should relax and just let whatever happens, happen.

But falling for this guy could really break me. Can I handle that on top of just losing my best friend? I'm sure there is only so much heartbreak a person can take, and I'm not the strongest person to begin with. There's always been something broken about me, can I handle more pain, more loss?

I pull the blanket around me and roll over to face the wall. My eyes flutter closed as my heart rate slows.

I'm almost asleep when he walks back into the room, crawling into bed behind me. He slides his left arm up under my pillow and pulls me against his chest while wrapping his right arm around my middle. His heat and scent flow over me like a soothing blanket, and I drift off into a peaceful sleep.

I WAKE in the morning to an empty bed. I wonder where he went, but don't worry long. I decide to slip into the shower to wake up.

When I step out, I dry off and pull on some clothes before walking back out into the room. River is unloading a brown, paper bag onto the bed.

"I figured you wouldn't want to go back over to that restaurant, so I ran over and got us breakfast."

I smile from his sweet gesture. "Thank you." I sit on the bed and he hands me a cup of coffee. I take a sip and the sweet mixture warms my throat.

"I didn't know what you wanted to eat, so I just got us both breakfast sandwiches."

"That's perfect. Thanks."

He sits down beside me and hands me a wrapped sandwich. There's an odd feeling that settles over me. Sitting here next to him in such an intimate setting, feeling like a normal couple, sets my skin on fire. Just yesterday I was trying to deny these feelings, and to be honest, I don't even know what these feelings are. I've never been in love. I'd had feelings for Nick at one point in time, but as time went by, we drifted apart before we ever really got close.

Love doesn't happen this fast, does it? I need to know

someone to love them, get to know their dreams and wants, get to know their soul, right?

"What are you thinking so hard about?" His voice cuts right through the silence and my inner turmoil.

I shake my head with a mouth full of food.

He sets his sandwich down and dusts the crumbs off his hands. "Are you having doubts?"

My eyes cut to him. "Doubts about what? The trip?"

He shakes his head slowly, looking a little nervous.

I know what he means now, doubts about us. I place my sandwich on my lap. "You mean about us?"

He nods, placing his elbows on his knees and leaning over, hanging his head like he's waiting for the ball to drop.

"River, I'm not doubting us because to me, there is no *us* to doubt. I don't know what we have. I'm confused. I have these feelings for you that I shouldn't have yet. I barely know you."

He turns to me, placing his hands on either side of my face while his eyes bore into mine. "How does it feel when we touch? When I kiss you, you don't pull away like you would with a complete stranger. There is an *us*. You just need to drop what society finds acceptable, because I belonged to you the moment your lips brushed against mine, when I didn't know any more than your name."

I not only hear his words, but I feel them too. They pool around me, seeping in through every crack in my shattered mindset. Having such strong feelings for this man so soon, may not be right by society's standards, but it's completely right for me. It's not perfect and it doesn't make any sense, but right now, he is exactly what I need.

I move my lips to his and plant a soft kiss against them. "You're right. Katie always said I needed to loosen up. What we have, it may not make sense, but it does feel right."

He moves to the floor on his knees, kneeling in front of me. His strong hands cup my face. "So let's get on with this trip and forget about society for a while." His lips land on mine firmly, full of assurance. He kisses me until I'm breathless and blinded by passion. When he pulls away and looks into my eyes with his ocean blue ones, my entire body erupts in tingles. I'm not ever going to get enough of him. He's cocky and self-assured, but he also reassures me and challenges me. Something I need more of with Katie gone.

His lips are red and glistening from our kiss. They're so warm and inviting. I want more, but I shake away the overwhelming need to be touched by him.

"Are you ready to pick up where we left off?"

I nod, still completely breathless from the kiss and the intense emotions that have been wreaking havoc on my fragile mind.

He stands and holds out his hand. I place mine in his and he pulls me up from the bed, my chest smashing against his as he holds me close.

His breath blows across my face as he says, "let's go."

AN HOUR LATER, we're back in the car, zooming down the interstate. I sit back letting the wind blow through my hair while River drives. The radio is up loud, blaring *Ho Hey* by *The Lumineers*, and I feel completely carefree as I sing along with the song.

Every now and then I catch him watching me from the corner of his eye before offering up a smirk. I poke his side as I sing the lyrics even louder. He laughs, making his blue eyes shine as he shakes his head at me.

I half way crawl into the backseat, riffling through his bag until I pull out the flask he'd produced on the day we met. He smacks me on the ass and I yelp. I take my seat next to him and show it to him. He waggles his eyebrows while his eyes rake over my body.

I feel my face flush under his stare, but I uncap the flask and take a long swallow. The familiar liquid burns my throat and warms a trail all the way down to my stomach.

He keeps looking at me, and I can't stop looking at him. He causes these feelings inside of me I've never felt before. For the first time in a long time, in this moment, I'm happy. I know Katie is smiling down on me. This list is doing everything she hoped it would. I'm stepping out of the shadows little by little. I'm having fun, and trying new things. And it's a fucking blast.

8

Start a Bar Fight

We drive for hours before we stop in another small town to grab some lunch. It's so nice outside that I can't bear to sit in a crowded restaurant. We run through a drive-through and find a nice, quiet park.

We sit at a picnic table while we eat. The sun is shining bright, warming my skin. A slight breeze blows, keeping me from getting too hot, and the soft rustling sound of the tree branches moving relaxes me. There is a small pond that has at least a dozen white ducks floating along the top. They look so cute. I've never been this close to ducks before. I've never really been close to any animal other than a dog or cat.

I see a squirrel run down a tree, and he runs across the

grass to another tree. I grab a french fry and toss it out onto the ground between the trees, almost to the water.

The squirrel stops what he's doing, looking around cautiously before he finally jumps down and rushes to the fry. He picks it up with his mouth and rushes back up the tree.

I giggle and throw another.

"I don't think that's a good idea," River says sitting across from me.

"What? Why? Do you think I'm going to be attacked by a squirrel?"

"No, I'm more concerned about those ducks." He uses his head to motion toward the water.

I look over and see that all the ducks have seen my exchange with the squirrel.

I smile. "I have plenty for them too." I grab a handful and toss them onto the ground. They move quickly to get the fries while squawking noisily.

When all the fries have disappeared from the ground, they all look at me angrily. I quickly throw another handful down to keep them busy.

"Wow. They must be starving."

"They're not starving. Ducks will eat anything. When I was a kid my mom used to take me to this one pond in the city to feed the ducks," he says before popping a fry into his mouth.

"Did you feed them french fries too?" I ask with a smile, happy he's telling me about his childhood.

He lets out a laugh. "No, we were pretty poor. I didn't even know what a french fry was until I was old enough to find food for myself."

His confession makes me a little sad. Is this why he's never volunteered much information about his past before?

"We didn't have a lot of money when I was growing up so I never got to do the things normal kids did. But the one thing I did get to do was going to that pond and feeding the ducks because it didn't require any money. If we had bread left at the end of the week, she would take me. I loved doing that with her. It was our time together. She worked all the time to provide the little she could. Just to make sure I got that time with her, I would eat sandwiches with only one slice just so we'd get our time together that week."

"Awe, it sounds like you were a sweet little boy. I'd love to meet her one da— Oww!" I turn and look to see what just caused the blinding pain in my side. A duck stands next to me, squawking, rearing back to bite me again.

River laughs. "They can be demanding little shits."

I toss more fries and it waddles away.

"You better make sure you save some for the walk back to the car or we'll be chased."

I hold up the fry container. "They're all gone."

He goes stock still as more ducks start moving in our direction.

"We better go." He stands and reaches for my hand as the mob nears us.

The ducks must have a sixth sense for this sort of thing

because it's like they all turn on us. I freeze, and they do too as they all stare at me. I swear I can see a shadow of fire dancing in their beady eyes like they all came directly from Hell.

"Let's go!" River tugs my arm as we rush towards the car with every last duck quacking and chasing after us. I laugh and squeal as we run with them on our heels.

We finally reach the car and I jump inside, slamming the door behind me. I'm clutching my chest and breathless when River jumps in beside me while the ducks surround the car.

"Fuck! One bit me on the ass!"

I roll in laughter, further impairing my ability to breathe.

"That fucking hurt." He lifts his ass off the seat and lowers his pants enough for me to see the pink, circular mark on his skin. The edges are already turning a light shade of blue.

I lift my shirt to reveal my side, and I have a mark matching his. "Oh my God. Those are Hell ducks!"

He lifts an eyebrow. "Hell ducks?"

"Yeah, they came directly from Hell! I thought ducks were friendly."

He pulls his pants back up and starts the car. "They are for the most part. They just fight for what they want. Nothing wrong with that."

"Haven't you ever heard the saying, don't bite the hand that feeds?"

He looks at me while pulling on his seatbelt. "I have, but do you want to go ask the ducks if they have?"

I narrow my eyes at him. "Get me away from these demon ducks."

"Oh, so now they're *demon* ducks?" He shifts into drive and pulls out slowly, avoiding the ducks that just won't give up.

"Oh, they're demon ducks alright. Fuck these ducks." I sit back and cross my arms over my chest.

As we pull away, I lift my hand and raise my middle finger.

"Are you seriously flipping off the ducks right now?" His voice is full of amusement.

I let my hand fall onto my lap. "No."

I hear his deep chuckle fill the car before we're driving away from the demon ducks, heading back towards the interstate.

As we're driving down the road, I pull the list from my bag and mark off 'send back a wrong order' and start looking for the next thing I can cross off.

"What's next?" River asks, breaking the silence.

I roll my eyes and let out a sigh. "I have no idea. I swear she did this just to watch me squirm."

"Why would you say that?"

"Perform a strip tease?" I say as I turn to look at him.

He grins from ear to ear. "I'd like to watch that."

I ignore him as I continue on down the list. "Give a guy a fake number?"

He quickly looks over at me. "How did she pick the things on that list?"

I take a deep breath and set the notebook in my lap. "It's all things I've never done. I'm not big on going out. I don't flirt with random guys or dance."

"I find it hard to believe that you never had to give a guy a fake number."

"I'm not very approachable, as Katie says." I push my dark hair away from my face as I slide my sunglasses on. "I don't know if I can do these things. I mean, yeah I can give a guy a fake number, but strip?" I feel my nerves shoot up just from thinking about it.

His hand lands on mine with a soft squeeze. "Don't worry about it now. We'll get you drunk first."

I slap his chest with a laugh. Grateful for him bringing me out of my sadness.

We drive for hours. My butt has long ago gone numb. I stare out the window and watch as we pass by nothing but trees. I sleep off and on and River just drives contently. He never complains about being stuck in the car, the traffic, or my lack of conversation. When I want to talk, he joins in, but when I start thinking about this trip and why I'm taking it, he's completely happy just sitting at my side, holding my hand.

I still don't know much about him, but we don't have

that awkwardness of needing to fill the silence with meaningless chit-chat. He doesn't feel like a stranger to me. We connect on some level I don't quite understand. I haven't had this instant connection with anyone other than Katie. Is it crazy to think Katie sent him to me? If I think about it, I only met him because of her. I never would have kissed him without her list. I never would have even talked to him if it wasn't for her. Is this what she was hoping would happen when making that list?

Thinking about her gives me this feeling of happiness, but also sadness. I miss her so much. I want to pick up the phone to tell her about River. I want to tell her how I'm checking items off her list. I want to tell her how much I love and miss her.

Without thinking, I grab the notebook and a pen and start to write her a letter. I know she won't ever read it, but I think just getting the words out will help. Isn't writing supposed to be therapeutic?

Katie,

God, how I miss you! There are days that I forget you're gone, and I pick up the phone to call you. That's when it hurts the most. I'm not so sure about that actually. It hurts all the time. I know this is a stupid idea, but maybe you really can see me right now. I hope so. I want you to see me doing all the things on your list. And I'm really hoping you're enjoying torturing me. I met a guy. His name is River. He's tall and blond. He has this six pack that makes me weak in the knees. (Yes, I used that term) I don't know much about him yet, but there is something about him that feels familiar. Something is happening between us, and I'm powerless to stop it, even when I try. He's fun, annoying, and drop dead sexy. But the best part, he doesn't ask me if I'm okay. He knows I'm not. Back home, that's all everyone would ask me. I got so tired of lying. Being out on the road with him, I don't have to lie. He understands why I'm hurting, and he doesn't try to make it better. He just accepts that I'm broken and doesn't try to put together my pieces, although he does help me forget that I'm missing so many. Anyway, I should probably go. I'm sure you're up in heaven right now, lounging on a cloud and being fed marshmallows by an angel with a six pack and biceps the size of my head.

I love you,

Jovi

I close the notebook and clutch it to my chest. I feel my eyes tear up from thinking that this is the only way I can talk to her now. I'll never see her face or hear her voice again. For the first week, I repeatedly called her cell just so I could hear the recording. Each and every time, it just made it worse for me. Katie was the glue that held me together, and now that she's gone, I'm falling to pieces.

I squeeze my eyes shut to keep the tears from falling. I try to calm my breathing and relax. My heart rate slows as I drift off into a deep sleep.

Katie and I are watching MTV in her living room when

her dad walks through the front door. He usually stops to say hi to us, but today, he walks straight through to the kitchen. After a couple minutes of quiet, the silence is broken when the sound of something crashing fills my ears.

"How could you not tell me about this?" Mary, Katie's mom, screams.

"Honey, please calm down. It was a long time ago. I didn't tell you because I didn't know there was anything to tell," George explains.

I look over at Katie and she rolls her eyes. "Who knows what they're fighting about now."

We're fifteen, but in this moment, she looks like a little girl who always gets afraid when her parents fight.

I know she needs me right now. I place my hand in hers and squeeze. "I'm sure everything will be okay. Do you want to go outside and take turns on the swing?"

She offers a small smile and nods before we stand and head out the front door.

"WAKE UP, SLEEPYHEAD. WE'RE HERE."

I jump awake and rub the sleep from my eyes. I look around us to find we're parked in a hotel parking lot. "Where are we?"

"Somewhere in Arizona." He removes the keys from the ignition and opens his door to step out.

"God, are we ever going to get out of this state?"

He opens the back door and grabs our bags. "Maybe if we don't stop every hour." His eyes narrow on me as wrinkles form at the edges.

"I'm sorry. I have to pee!"

We both walk around the car and he wraps his arm around my shoulders. "Let's check in and then we'll find some place to eat."

We find a bar and grill and take a seat as we wait on a waitress. The place is crowded and appears to be more of a bar than a grill. There are pool tables, dart boards, and a jukebox, along with a big stage and dance floor. The front of the building was lined with motorcycles and all the bikers are gathered at the bar. They are loud and rowdy, but I try to ignore them as I look over the menu.

The jukebox kicks on, playing *Pour Some Sugar on Me*, and River leans back, placing his arm across the bench seat. "So how about that strip show?" He winks at me.

I laugh out loud. "No way! We'd be kicked out. Plus, I don't want those fat, hairy bikers drooling all over me. I'm not so sure you could take them."

He scoffs. "I'm not worried about them."

I nod with a fake smile, not so sure.

We eat and stick around to have a few drinks, just enjoying being out of the car. The bar continues to fill with people and it's growing louder and louder.

At ten, the main lights shut off and the bar dims. Black lights come on just as someone takes the stage. I turn to watch, hoping for a live band, but to my surprise, it's karaoke.

I shrink down into my seat as River turns quickly to look at me, excitement written on his face. "How perfect is this?"

"Not happening, dude." I shake my head.

"Waitress! Another round!" he shouts.

I'm still not agreeing. "No fucking way."

"Why not? You don't know these people." He motions around the bar with a wave of his hand. "You'll never see them again."

I sit upright and lean across the table. "I thought we were just having dinner and drinks, not worrying about the list right now."

"We were, but when the opportunity comes along…"

The waitress places our drinks on the table and River hands over the money.

"I'll be right back," he says, standing.

I latch onto his hand like if he leaves me sitting alone I might die. "Where are you going?"

He shakes free from my grasp. "Chill. I'm just going to the bathroom."

I sink back, sipping my drink.

The song ends and the DJ's voice takes over the bar. "Give a round of applause for Nikki!" The bar breaks out with people clapping and cheering. "Next up, Joooviieee."

I sit up straight as River comes walking back to the table

with a shit-eating grin. He reaches for me, but I dodge away.

"No fucking way."

He grabs me and pulls me up. "Come on, Jovie. You have to cross it off your list sometime."

"But why now? Why not tomorrow?"

He laughs in my ear, his breath blowing across my heated skin. "You're always going to say tomorrow, but tomorrow isn't promised." He walks me to the stage and practically pushes me up the two steps.

I turn and look at all the eyes on me. I freeze like a deer caught in the headlights as I'm handed a microphone. The music starts up to *Closer* by The Chainsmokers ft. Halsey.

With all eyes on me, I can't do it. I can't sing. I miss the beginning of the vocals and don't know how to jump in. My eyes flash nervously around the crowd. They're all staring at me, waiting for me to sing, but I don't even know how to use my voice right now.

I'm about to drop the microphone and run off stage when River's voice comes over the speakers, filling the bar. He walks up on the stage, singing the song for me.

He walks up to my side and takes my hand while singing directly to me. My face heats up with all eyes on us. He turns us so my back is to the crowd and every time I try to turn away from him, he directs me back to his eyes. I know it's his own little way of telling me to focus only on him and not the crowd. When the chorus comes around, he lifts my hand that's still holding the microphone at my side and raises it to my lips.

I start singing along with him, but my voice is shaking and full of nerves. He places his hand on the base of my neck and pulls me closer, never missing a beat of the song. The closer he gets to me, the further away the crowd gets. My voice grows stronger as I sing along.

When the song wraps up, I've completely forgotten all about the crowd. It was just me and him up here, singing to one another. The rush I feel when the crowd cheers makes my face burn with embarrassment.

River bows, eating up the attention, before leading me from the stage.

I try my best to hide my face from the crowd as we walk through to the bar.

"You were amazing, beautiful." His lips land against mine and it only fuels the rampant emotions pumping through me.

When he pulls away, we're both breathless. "Check that off your list. I'll be right back."

I'm so lost in my thoughts, I don't even think to stop him, but he better not do that to me again.

I order us a round of drinks just as a big biker stops at my side. "Hi, gorgeous." The tip of his wide nose is slightly red, along with his ears. I can tell from looking at him that he is three sheets to the wind.

"Hi." I smile, hoping that's all he's seeking and will leave me alone.

"Did you come here with someone?"

I nod. "Yeah, he just went to use the restroom."

The bartender places our drinks in front of me and I hand over some cash. I grab the drink and take a sip, hoping the biker at my side takes the hint that I don't want to talk.

"Me and my buddies are about to head out. You ever rode on a real man's bike before?"

I snort in laughter. "No, I can honestly say I haven't."

I see River walk out of the bathroom from over the bikers shoulder. Thank God.

"Do you want to?"

I scrunch up my nose. "Not tonight, but thank you," I reply, trying to be polite and not start trouble.

"Can I get your number then? Maybe tomorrow." What a persistent little shit.

Lightbulb! "Sure."

He hands me a napkin and pulls a pen from his leather vest.

I write down a fake number and slide it across the bar. He looks cocky as he picks it up and folds it in half. "I look forward to talking to you again."

I smile and nod. *Yeah right, guy. You're never going to hear from me again.*

Before he turns to walk away, he wraps his big arm around my shoulders and pulls me in for a kiss. His mustache rubs against my face as his fat, wet lips press against mine.

I'm in complete shock. My eyes are wide open while

I'm completely frozen. River's eyes land on mine and he sees the panic written in them.

"Hey!" He pulls the big man away from me.

The man doesn't even say anything. He just swings, connecting with River's jaw.

One hit was all it took. The whole atmosphere of the bar changes. Everyone saw the exchange and it seems to give them the permission they needed to hit any person who's annoyed them all night.

I stand stunned as a huge fight breaks out all around me. River is throwing punches at the biker, landing one after another. And somehow, he tosses the man down long enough to grab my wrist and pull me towards the exit. Just as we're running through the door, a beer bottle flies behind me, shattering off the wall and I duck instinctively, heart hammering.

We rush to the car and the people fighting seem to trickle out with us.

When the cops speed into the parking lot, we kick up dust leaving fast.

"What the fuck happened?" he asks me with blood dripping from his lip.

I smile with realization. "I get to cross off *three* things."

"Sing karaoke, give out a fake number, and what?" he asks, his eyes glancing from the road to me and back.

"Start a bar fight!" I pull the list from my bag and cross off three more.

9
Go Camping

"I THINK *I* WAS THE ONE THAT STARTED THE BAR FIGHT," River insists as his face lights up from the oncoming traffic.

My mouth hangs open. "What? It was over me!"

"But I was the one who hit the guy," he argues.

"Well if you want to get technical, he hit *you* first. And since it was all over me, *I* started the bar fight." I smile, full of excitement, embarrassment, and maybe feeling a little shameless.

He lets the subject drop as we quietly drive back to the hotel.

When we get back, I grab a bucket of ice and put some in a towel. I crawl up on his lap and hold it on his jaw. "It's already starting to bruise," I say, lightly trailing a finger across the purple bruise forming on his jaw.

It feels like everything around us quietens as he looks up at me with sincere eyes. "It's alright. I'd do it all over again for you."

I feel myself blush. "Did he hit hard?" I ask, keeping the ice on his jaw, the simple touch making my stomach tighten with the fire burning inside of me.

"The guy was easily two-hundred and fifty pounds. Yeah, he hit pretty hard!"

I look down and see that his black and blue flannel shirt had all the buttons ripped off the front from the fight. "Awe, your shirt is ruined too. I love this shirt on you." The various shades of blue and teal contrasting with the black, makes his eyes pop. I run my hand down his chest where the row of buttons should be.

When I look back up, his eyes are clouded over as his lips find mine. I'm totally lost in our kiss when he pulls away. "So, be honest, who's a better kisser, me or that biker?"

I smack his shoulder, my hand slipping to hit his bruised jaw.

"Ow!" he calls out while I apologize around my giggles.

"Yeah, you seem real sorry." He stands, holding me in his arms, against his chest as he spins us around. He lays me on the bed and starts crawling up my body. "Since I've met you, I've been bitten in the ass by a duck, and I got into a bar fight."

I run my hands under his shirt, my fingers gliding across

his washboard abs. "I think you need to toughen up if you're going to be hanging out with me."

He pauses on top of me like he's surprised by what I said. "Oh yeah? You're just another rebel without a cause, huh?" He lifts himself up to his knees, pulling off his shirt.

I bite my bottom lip and nod, trying to hide my smile.

IT TAKES A FEW MORE DAYS, but we're finally half way to Miami. I haven't tried to cross anything else off the list, not after all the trouble it got us into the last time. We drive all day, stopping only for gas and bathroom breaks. Then when the sun begins to set, we find a small town to crash for the night.

We just made it to Kennard, Texas and, instead of staying in another boring hotel, we stop at an outdoor store to grab some camping supplies.

I'm a city girl and have never camped in my life, but River says it's something I need to do, even if it's not on the list.

We pay for one night in the Davy Crockett National Forest and set up camp.

River gets to work starting a fire while I read the directions to put up the tent.

"Think you can manage?" he asks over his shoulder.

"Think you can manage to not burn down the whole forest?" I shoot back.

He flips me off before turning to his work.

I giggle as I start pulling pieces out of the bag. I follow along with the directions, laying the tent out flat, and then move on to piecing together the poles. I lay the poles across the top of the tent like the picture shows and step back, looking at it.

There are three poles lying on top of the tent. Two make a big X and the other lies across the X horizontally. It's just like the picture.

"What's wrong?" he asks, dropping his pile of wood in the fire pit.

I spin around to face him. "How does it pop up?"

He cocks his head to the side and draws his brows together. "How does what pop up?"

I pick up the bag the tent was in and show it to him. "It says pop up tent. I laid everything out just like the picture shows, but how do you get it to pop up?"

His eyes flash from me, to the picture of the tent on the bag, and then to the tent lying flat on the ground. "Wait. You expect the tent to just pop up? Like, on its own?"

"Well yeah! Why else would it be called a pop up tent?"

His laughter cuts through me. I smile, not sure what's so funny. When he begins to calm down, he looks at me and it just starts all over again.

It's starting to get annoying. "Why are you laughing?"

"You..." More laughing. "...think... the tent..." He stops talking while more laughter escapes him. "...is going to just *pop* up?" When he says the word 'pop' his hand goes from a fist to all his fingers outstretched like an explosion.

I cross my arms over my chest. "Would you stop fucking laughing and tell me what's so damn funny? Does it not pop up like it says?"

He's clutching his side from laughing so hard. Tears are streaming down his bright red face. I'm sure my face is growing red from anger.

"Can I help you folks?" a park ranger asks as he walks up on our camping site.

River points at him "Ask him your question."

I turn to the ranger in annoyance. "My stupid boyfriend bought this pop-up tent. I followed the directions exactly. See?" I show him the paper with the images on it. "Why isn't it popping up?" I suddenly realize that I just called River my boyfriend. Panic sets in, but when I turn and look back at him, he's still so busy laughing that he didn't catch it. Thank God!

River is still rolling as the ranger does the same thing he did. He looks at me, the picture, and then the tent. "You do realize that those poles slide into the pockets to pop it open, don't you?"

River stops to take a breath. "No, she thinks it just *pops...*" he does the hand gesture again. "...open, like on its own."

The ranger chuckles, causing River to start all over again.

I tug the paper out of his hands and move back to the

tent. How was I supposed to fucking know? I've never put together a tent before. If something says pop up, it should fucking pop up!

I slide the poles into the little pockets I hadn't seen before and little by little, the tent starts to pop up. I feel embarrassment wash over me.

AFTER THE FIRE is going and the tent "pops up," River and I are sitting around the burning logs, cooking hotdogs on sticks, something else I've never done.

"So did you camp a lot as a kid?" I ask, just wanting to know more about him.

"No, my mom couldn't take the time off work to go. Plus, camping requires a lot of stuff we didn't have."

I have a feeling I shouldn't ask, but I do. "What about your dad? Were they divorced?"

"No, they were never married. My dad knocked my mom up and refused to be a part of our lives."

"Have you ever met him?"

"Yeah, I've met him. When my mom got sick, I showed up at his house to ask for some money. I figured it was the least he could do, he has plenty of it. It's not like he stuck around to help raise me. I figured giving away money would be easy for him, unlike giving a shit about me and my mom."

"What happened?"

"He told me to get off his property before his new family came home and caught me there. Didn't give me a fucking dime."

I feel my heart crumble for him. "What was wrong with your mom?"

He rubs the light scruff on his jaw. "Um, she was diagnosed with lung cancer. She never was a smoker, but she waitressed in restaurants that allowed smoking and she worked in clubs and bars. She was always around it. I remember her coming home smelling of smoke so bad it burned my eyes when I hugged her." His Adam's apple bobs in this throat. I can see how much talking about this hurts him.

"I'm sorry for asking. You don't push me to talk about Katie, I didn't mean to push you."

He pulls the hotdog out of the fire and places it on a bun. "You didn't force me. I like sharing things with you. I just don't want to give away all my secrets just yet and break the spell for you." He smiles after quoting his words from before.

"Here." He hands me the hotdog. "Let me know what you think about your first roasted hotdog."

I take it and study it, making sure it's not covered in soot or dirt or anything living.

"It's not going to hurt you. Just try it," he urges.

I take a deep breath and close my eyes to take a big bite.

"Without the teeth, that's a nice image," he jokes.

I lean over and smack him while chewing and swallowing.

"So?"

I nod with a smile. "It's not bad."

"Not bad?" He scoffs. "Just wait until you try the s'mores."

"I've had s'mores."

He puts another hotdog on the stick. "But have you had them made on an open fire, not in a microwave?"

"No, I guess not."

"Did you spend your life under a rock?" he teases.

I laugh. "Kind of."

We spend the rest of the night eating our hotdogs and s'mores, which are amazing. I discover I like them much more than microwave s'mores. I love them burnt to a crisp: when the outer shell peels off.

I also learn more about River. He doesn't realize this, but the more I come out of the shadows, the more he shows himself to me. The real him. The person he used to be, the reason he is the way he is, and I love him even more for it.

He pours a bucket of water on the fire before we crawl into the tent and below the sleeping bag.

The wildlife goes on around us. It's relaxing hearing the crickets chirp and the soft sounds of the water rippling. The smell of the wet earth is all around us, mixing with the scent of the pine trees. River's deep, rich scent mixes perfectly with our wooded surroundings.

I roll over to face him, and I place my hand on his

angular jaw, tilting his head to the side to meet my stare. "Thank you for telling me a little about your life."

He moves, placing his arm behind my head, bringing me closer against his body. "You don't have to thank me. I'll make you a deal."

"What deal?" I look up at him wide eyed.

"Each time you mark something off your list, I'll tell you something about my past. It might not be something big or dramatic, but just a memory or something that has affected me in some way."

"Deal!" I move my mouth to his and he kisses me softly.

He slowly rolls us until I'm on my back and he's on his side, facing me. His right hand runs down my arm, latching onto my wrist before he pulls it above my head.

He pulls his left arm out from under my head and does the same until he's holding me down by my wrists. His lips find mine as he positions himself between my legs that are quivering with need for him.

"Are you going to hold me down?" I whisper against his lips while I move my hips against him.

"We're in the wilderness now, princess. It brings out the animal in me." His mouth covers mine as he demands entrance.

This, right here, reminds me of our night behind the club. The way he could go from cute boy-next-door to the dark, sexy, demanding predator at the flip of a switch.

His hot lips trail down my neck while his hands get busy pushing my oversized t-shirt up my thighs, revealing my hot pink panties. His hand runs over my sex and it sends a chill through me. "You're soaking your panties, beautiful." He tugs them down my legs. "Let's just get rid of these."

The moment they are pulled off, his mouth finds me. His tongue runs across my slit, over the hard nub, making me buck with pleasure. My hand tangles in his hair, not allowing him to move.

He lets out a small laugh, his breath blowing across the wet junction between my legs, and it only makes me want him more.

His big hands wrap around my thighs while he doubles his efforts. The tent fills with the sounds of my heavy breathing and the sounds of him licking and sucking my clit into his mouth. Just as I'm about to let my release go, he thrusts into me, making me come undone around him. Every muscle tightens with my orgasm. I'm squeezing him so hard he can barely move inside of me. He pulls out all he can before pushing back in.

Pure ecstasy has been released inside of me. I don't think anything of it when I roll him over and take my place on top of him. My fingers are splayed out across his shirtless chest as I ride every inch of him. He fits me perfectly, stretching just enough to add a little pain, but in a good way.

I open my eyes to see his face contorted with pleasure. His brows are pulled together and he's biting his bottom lip. His hands hold me by my thighs as he lifts me up and pulls me back down as hard and quickly as he can.

My head falls back as my lips part with a loud moan.

My eyes flutter closed. I'm no longer in control of my body. It's purely primal now. I shatter into a million pieces as he lets out a groan and fills me with my muscles clenching around him.

I feel him shudder inside of me before I slide off of him, to his side. I rest my head against his chest, listening as his breathing and heart go crazy for me.

"I'm sorry I didn't last long. When you rolled me over and rode my dick, I was about to come right then."

I giggle from hearing his words. "I'm glad I finally pushed *you* to break."

He rolls to cover my body with his as he looks deeply into my eyes. "I've been broken for a long time, princess. I fucking shattered when I met you." His lips crash against mine again, and before I know it, he's back inside of me, breaking me to pieces and putting them back together.

I WAKE in the early morning with my back aching. I open my eyes to the sun filled tent and groan. Why did I think camping was a good idea?

I reach for River but he's gone. I sit up, pulling on my clothes, and step out. He's up moving around the campsite, packing things away while cooking something over the fire.

"Good morning." He places a kiss on my forehead.

"What are you cooking? And do you have any coffee?" I ask, blocking the sun from my eyes as I watch him move around with more energy than anyone should have at this ungodly hour.

"Eggs and bacon, and yes, there is coffee."

I sit down on a big rock next to the fire pit. "Where'd you get coffee?"

"They have a concession stand." He hands me a paper cup before plopping down beside me. He picks up a spatula and uses it to flip the eggs.

"How do you know so much about camping and cooking like this if you never went as a kid?" I take a sip of my coffee, attempting to wake up.

He looks at me with a wicked gleam in his eyes. "I can only tell you if you cross something off your list."

I scoff. "Like what? What can I cross off right here in the middle of the woods?"

"Go skinny dipping."

Fuck, I forgot that was on there. I look around at the tents that are fairly close to ours, but it's so early, nobody is up yet.

I stand without argument and pull my shirt over my head.

"Really? You're just going to do it without a fight?"

I toss the shirt in his face. "It's too early to argue." As I walk down the bank, I wiggle out of my shorts and panties. He stands from his spot by the fire and watches with a big grin covering his face.

I rush into the cool water and as soon as I'm deep enough, jump below the surface. The cold water helps to cool my overheated body that's burning with embarrassment. I swim underwater until I can no longer hold my breath. I break the surface, panting for much needed oxygen.

I swim back to shore, watching him the whole way. He hasn't moved a muscle.

I step out of the water and grab my clothes as I walk back toward him, as naked as the day I was born. When I'm standing at his side, holding out my hand for my shirt, I ask, "Did you enjoy the view?"

He smiles a boyish grin. "I did. I think the rest of the camp did too." He uses his thumb to get my attention to the rows of tents surrounding ours.

I glance around to see three men, belonging to three different camping parties, watching me with their mouths hanging open.

I scream and dash for the tent while River's laugh cuts through the silence.

While I'm inside trying to calm my racing heart, I hear a loud whistle before River yells, "alright guys, show's over!"

I'm sooo going to get him back for that.

10
Perform a Striptease

WHEN I STEP OUT OF THE TENT, FULLY DRESSED, THE MEN that were gathered around give me a round of applause. I force a smile and wave like it doesn't bother me, but I can feel the heat escaping my face from embarrassment and anger.

I take a seat next to River as he pulls the food off the fire. "You're so dead."

He looks at me with his mouth agape. "What? I didn't plan for that to happen."

"Mm-hmm. I think you owe me something."

He hands over my plate that I sit in my lap. I don't move to eat it until he opens his mouth to talk.

"What was the question? How do I know so much about camping?"

I nod slowly while bringing a piece of bacon to my mouth.

He takes a deep breath. "I know a lot about camping because I used to be homeless. After my mom passed away and before I managed to get a job in advertising, I lived just like this." He motions towards our camp.

I swallow before dropping my bacon on my plate. "How'd you manage to get a job like that if you were homeless?"

"Pure fucking luck," he answers around a mouthful of bacon. He finishes chewing and swallows. "I bumped into this guy one night, and he was fucked up. He said he had only had a few drinks, but someone must have slipped him something. That or he was lying. Either way, I didn't care. I drove his car to his house and helped him get inside. I was going to leave, but he got sick and I was worried he was going to choke to death on his own vomit." He shrugs. "So I stayed and cleaned him up, made sure he didn't die. The next morning, he was so thankful, he offered me a job and a place to stay until I saved up enough money."

"Wow. That's crazy." I resume eating.

He nods. "Yeah, he was a great guy. We got to be really good friends over the six months I lived there."

"What happened to him? Is he still a big-wig in New York?"

Slowly, he shakes his head. "No, he O.D'd. He was living alone because he was going through a divorce. His wife packed up their two kids and moved out of the state without even telling him. He just came home one day, and they were gone. Left a fucking note." His jaw clenches in anger. "Anyway, he was severely depressed and drank and did a lot of drugs to cope. He lived for work, and once we became friends, he got better. We hung out a lot and kept each other's mind off shit, but I never should have moved out. Leaving him alone with his demons like that…" He pulls his eyes away from mine, looking into the fire. "It just ate him alive. I wasn't there to stop it that time."

What's left of my heart explodes into so many tiny pieces, there's nothing but dust left.

"Oh my God. I'm so sorry." I feel tears sting my eyes, but I hold them back. I wish I could have made his life better for him. He's helped me so much since Katie's passing. I wonder if he saw something in me that day, something that reminded him of his friend. I want to ask, but I don't know if I can stand to talk about it anymore. I know it will only hurt him.

"It's okay. I did all I could. I didn't know he would start using. I mean, we drank and had a good time on occasion, but he'd never do drugs, that I saw." His eyes find mine again. "I couldn't have lived there forever."

I nod, completely understanding.

"Not a day goes by that I don't thank him though. He saved me from the streets, he brought me into his house, just a random homeless guy. For all he knew, I could have stolen all his shit. But he trusted me. He gave me a job. I wouldn't be who I am today without him."

"He was your Katie," I say, looking at him from under my lashes.

"He was my Katie," he repeats with a wink in my direction.

ONCE WE PILE everything back into the car, I dig my list out and cross off 'go skinny dipping'. My face flushes again just from thinking about the embarrassing mishap.

It's still early, so the heat of the day hasn't set in yet. I roll my window down and crank the music. *Howlin' for You* by The Black Keys plays loudly over the speakers. I look at River and see him mouthing the words along with the song. I smile, getting to see him so happy and carefree makes my heart flutter.

I lean the seat back just a bit and close my eyes while the warm morning air blows through the car and through my mess of long, dark hair.

River reaches over and takes my hand in his. He lifts it up and presses a kiss on the top before letting it fall beside me. I smile at him without opening my eyes, knowing that he saw it. This trip is doing things to me I never expected. The more I learn about him, the more I fall in love with him.

My eyes pop open as that thought crosses my mind.

"What's the matter?" he asks over the music.

"Nothing." I act like nothing is wrong, but something is wrong. I'm falling in love with this guy. How could that have happened? The last thing I knew, he annoyed me and was driving me up the fucking wall.

I know I let my guard down just to see what happened between us, but I never in a million fucking years expected this.

This can't be happening. I mean, in a perfect world we would take this trip together, fall madly in love and never look back. But in this world, the one where the people you love and care about the most are stolen from you, it doesn't work like that. I can see it play out now: I fall in love, he takes whatever he wants from me, when we get back home, he acts like nothing happened, and then he's gone. Leaving me alone with a completely mangled heart.

I have to get a grip on whatever this is I'm feeling. It can't be love, it can't be. Maybe I'm just clinging to him because of the massive hole inside of me from losing Katie. Maybe, it's just friendship mixed with the attraction I feel for him. Whatever it is, needs to be figured out soon and stopped. At least until we have some clarity and can talk about what this means to the both of us.

I take a deep breath to calm myself and look at him. He's driving, completely lost in his own thoughts. He didn't see the little mental freak out I just had.

I adjust my seat back into the sitting position and pick up the notebook to write to Katie.

Katie,

God, I wish you were here. I need someone to talk to about this. I think I'm falling in love. Either that, or I have a brain aneurysm. You've been in love, you can tell me how it feels. But you're not here, and I don't know how to figure it out without you. When he looks at me, my heart pounds wildly, my palms get all sweaty, and it feels like a rock is stuck in my throat. I can't swallow it down. When he touches me, I see stars. For fuckin' real! I know all this sounds stupid, but I can't control these feelings. They're too strong. And you know what? They feel so good, I don't know if I want to control them. But what if he breaks my heart? My heart is already broken from losing you. I can't lose him too. Anyway, enough with my whining. Please tell me you're up there enjoying an endless open bar and having mind-blowing sex. I couldn't stand it if I thought you were unhappy. You deserve the best, all heaven and Earth have to offer.

I love you,

Jovi

I close the book and tuck it away in my purse. I'm still thinking about what these feeling are when River's voice cuts through my thoughts.

"So what's the plan when we get to Miami?"

I almost jump from the silence being suddenly broken. "What do you mean?"

"I mean it's going to get pretty expensive staying in a

hotel every night. Were you planning on renting an apartment or something?"

"Oh. I have no idea. I was just focusing on getting there."

Instead of being annoyed that I dropped the ball, he lets out a deep laugh.

"I'll start looking for something." I pull out my phone and look at places to rent for the summer.

By night fall, we still haven't made it out of Texas. We find a motel for the night and as soon as we walk in the door, I call the shower.

I drop my bag on the bed as I pass by and go directly to the bathroom. I feel nasty after camping last night without a shower, plus my plunge into the lake didn't help matters any.

I'm also looking forward to a little alone time. I need to sort through my feelings. Everything feels so right, but also completely fucked. I feel like I've been setting myself up for heartache this whole time.

I turn the shower on as hot as it will go and step beneath the stream. I let the water flow over my hair and body before turning around and resting my head against the shower wall.

"What's the matter?" River says from behind me.

I jump and spin around. "Fuck. Why do you keep doing

this to me?" I'm feeling too much emotion. I'm needing space, time to sort through everything going on inside my head.

"What are you talking about?" he asks, confused.

"Getting in the shower with me when I didn't invite you. I mean, is a little alone time too much to ask for?"

He looks like I've slapped him in the face as he holds his hands up in defeat. "I'm sorry. I thought after all we've been through it wasn't that big of a deal." He opens the door and steps out.

The bathroom door slams closed and I jump like it just hit me in the heart. In a way, I guess it kind of did.

Maybe I'm overreacting. I shouldn't have been angry with him. I think I'm letting everything pile up on top of me and it's beginning to weigh me down again. I need to talk to him, tell him this wasn't his fault.

I turn off the shower and wrap a towel around me. When I walk back into the room, he's nowhere to be found.

I feel my shoulders slump with disappointment. Great, now look what I've done.

Pushing it all from my mind, I walk back into the bath-room and finish with my shower. When I'm done, he still isn't back. I pull on a pair of jeans and a tank top, leaving my wet hair hanging down my back, and walk out. I need to find him. I have to tell him that I'm sorry, that none of this is his fault.

I remember seeing a bar only a block down the road. I'll try there first.

When I walk in, loud music pumps through the bar. The bass is so loud I can feel it vibrating through my chest. I squeeze through the crowd and look over every face I pass. I walk by the bar, but he's not sitting on a stool. I start my journey deeper into the building.

At the back of the bar is a small stage with three poles in the center. There are two girls up, swinging around, but no exotic dancers, thank God.

I push through until I see him out of the corner of my eye. He's sitting in the darkened corner booth. The multicolored lights flash over his face and his dark eyes meet mine. They are cold and unmoving, instantly sending a chill through me.

I take a deep breath and push on. I freeze when I see his arm wrapped around the back of the booth with a blonde on each side of him. He's not touching them, or even looking at them, but they are eating him with their eyes.

I angrily stomp over to him. "What are you doing? Why'd you leave?"

He looks at each girl next to him and gives me his cocky grin. "You didn't want me around." He shrugs carelessly. "Figured I'd find someone who does. And what do you know?" He leans forward, the grin never leaving his lips. "I found two."

"Find your own way home, pig." I turn on my heels and walk away from him.

I mean to leave, but I'm so angry I can't. I need a drink. I know it's going to go one of two ways. It will make me numb and help me forget, or it will intensify everything and make me pissed. But right now, I'm willing to take my chances because I haven't even allowed myself to love him yet, and already I hurt.

I take a seat on the barstool and order the largest Long Island Iced Tea they have. Luckily for me, they have fishbowl style drinks.

The bartender places my drink in front of me with four straws. I hand him some money, and grab three straws and toss them on the bar.

My lips don't leave the straw as I sit and stew in my anger. But slowly, over the course of an hour of continuous drinking, everything falls away.

It's going on midnight when a loud voice booms through the bar. "Please welcome Kandi, Mindi, and Lilli!"

The bar goes completely dark before a bright, white light pops on, pointing directly at the stage. *Pour Some Sugar on Me* by Def Leppard blares through the speakers as three women take to the stage.

The crowd goes wild with cheers as they stand by their poles. Suddenly, they all break out in a dance routine that consists of spinning around, humping the floor, and removing articles of clothing.

I watch completely mystified. How do these women do it? How do you have enough self-esteem to get up there in front of all these people and dance around while naked? And how the fuck do they make it look so easy?

It occurs to me that River is probably in heaven right

now. I spin and look in his direction. Before the large crowd was blocking my view of him, but now they are all pushed closer to the stage, clearing the way.

My eyes land on him, and he's not moving or talking. He's just watching me while the women on either side chatter away with each other. His arms are no longer outstretched behind them either. They appear to be sitting in his lap, still as a statue.

The fact that he's not touching them and they're not touching him makes me feel a little better, but him being over there with them still makes me as jealous as can be.

I spin around in my anger and down some more of my drink as another dance starts up.

"Hey!" I yell at the bartender once my drink is almost completely gone.

"I can't serve you another one of those," he says automatically when he sees my empty drink with only one straw.

I giggle and shake my head. "No. How can I do that?" I ask, pointing towards the stage.

"You want to dance?" His voice is full of surprise.

"Yeah. I *need* to actually."

He looks me up and down. "Fill out this waiver and let me copy your license."

"Really? That easy?"

He nods. "We go through a lot of girls. I've shortened the employment questions," he says with a smile.

Sounds legit.

I slide over my license and start filling out the paper. When he brings it back to me, he asks, "What's your stage name?"

I didn't think about that part. "River," I answer. I know the announcer saying his name will make him pay attention. It's my turn to make him jealous.

He sticks out his bottom lip and shrugs. "Alright. The ladies dressing room is straight back that way. I'll turn your name into the announcer. Any song you have in mind?"

Song. Song. What's a good stripping song? I shrug. "Surprise me."

I hop off the barstool and my vision blurs. I sure am glad I'm drunk right now because I'd never do this if I wasn't. But it's something I need to do. I need to cross it off.

I stumble into the changing room to find a bunch of naked women.

A red head stands up right. "Did Mick hire a newbie already? Fuck, Tiffini just quit not even an hour ago."

"I'm not hired. I'm just checking something off my bucket list."

They all laugh or smile with curious, and suddenly friendly, eyes.

The red head walks over to me. "You need something to wear?"

I look at my jeans and tank top. "Yeah, I guess I do."

"Come with me." She leads me to the back of the room where a large wall is covered with a curtain. She pulls it back, revealing the 'uniforms.'

"You're kind of late so all the good ones are probably taken, but I'm sure we can find you something."

She pulls out a school girl uniform: a short, white, collared shirt, a tiny, plaid skirt, and a red sting bikini underneath it.

"I have the white stockings and heels if you want." She hands over the skimpy outfit.

"That would be great. Thanks!" I smile wide, completely confused as to why.

This isn't something I want to do. Or is it?

Oh fuck it. Why even bother trying to figure out these emotions anymore?

I pull on the uniform that barely covers my ass and put on the heels. The girls make a fuss, pretending like I'm their personal Barbie. They deck me out in full on makeup and body glitter. I cringe when they rub the glitter over my skin and have second thoughts. I hate glitter with a passion.

Refusing to look at myself in the mirror, I push the feeling of wanting to vomit down and give myself a mental pep talk.

You can do this. Do it to get back at River. Do it for the list and Katie. No, do it for yourself. Put yourself out there, try new things. Live!

"You're up, sugar," the redhead says as the three girls, from the stage, rush into the dressing room, covering their bodies with the clothes they have shed.

"Everyone welcome the pretty Rivverr," Comes the announcement and I freeze.

The music starts up to Believer by Imagine Dragons. If I wasn't so nervous, I'd laugh at the song choice.

My hair is still down, but now that it has air dried, it hangs around me in loose curls. I use it to hide as much of my face as I can. I walk to the center pole and grab hold, not daring to look at River straight away.

I have no idea what to do, so I allow myself to loosen up and swing around it. As I feel more at ease, I look to my left where River is no longer sitting with the women, but standing at the side of the stage, watching with amusement and a smile playing on his lips.

I swing around the pole and dance to the song, but not as graphically as the other women did. I don't even know how to move like that. I figure as long as I lose *some* clothes, nobody will be complaining.

I offer a naughty grin as my fingers go to the buttons on my shirt, slowly unbuttoning each one as the crowd gets louder and louder. When the shirt is off, revealing my red, shiny bikini top, I drop the shirt onto the stage.

I do the same routine until I'm in nothing but the G-string. Ever so slowly, I peel them from my body and sling them at River just as the song wraps us.

The place goes dark as I make my way off stage in a hurry.

When I push through the door, I'm filled with nerves and excitement. I'm completely out of my element and loving the high it's giving me.

I pull my clothes back on and toss the 'uniform' into the dirty bin before telling the lady that helped me thank you.

I don't know what River is going to say or if he's still mad at me, but I don't stick around to find out. I make a bee-line for the door.

I walk as quickly as I can and don't stop or look behind me until I'm back in the motel room alone.

11
Paying River Back

Now that I'm alone, my heart slams against my chest, only pumping more anxiety through me. I can't believe I did that! I sit on the edge of the bed to calm myself down.

The stress of the day and the amount of alcohol I'd drunk is wearing on me. I decide to finally undress and crawl into bed, glitter and all. I'll deal with the consequences tomorrow. I stand and kick my jeans off, I'm about to pull my shirt over my head when the door opens and slams shut.

I turn my head in the direction of the noise. River walks in wearing a wide smile. He's rushing towards me with his arms held out at his side like he's going to hug me. This is not the response I wanted. I wanted him as jealous and as mad as I was.

When he's in arm's length, I reach out and smack him across the face.

He's stunned as he rubs his bruised jaw. "What the hell was that for?"

"What the hell were you doing at that bar with those women?"

He thinks it over before he smirks. "I wasn't with those women. They are the girlfriends of a couple of the dancers. They don't like leaving them sitting alone because they get hit on all night. Trust me, you are more their type than I am."

My face wrinkles with disgust. "Don't lie. I saw how they were looking at you."

He moves closer, but I step away, not wanting to be confused by his touch because I know my body will give into him.

He holds his hands up in front of him, palms facing me. "I swear, it was nothing."

"So you weren't trying to make me jealous?"

His hands fall at his sides. "No, I was just trying to get out of here to give you space. I know you won't say anything, but I can tell you're freaking out."

I let out a long breath of anxiety. "I'm sorry. I feel bad for treating you the way I did. I'm just so confused by everything, and we're moving fast. Like really fast." I fall to the edge of the bed, resting my elbows against my knees while drooping my head forward.

He sits beside me, but he doesn't touch me, which I'm thankful for.

"Look. I'm sorry. I was mad, but not because of what you said. I was mad because I thought things were changing with us. I thought you were finally letting me beneath all your layers, finally letting me in."

"I am and that scares the shit out of me. I didn't even mean to let my guard down this much. You just wormed your way in and that scares me."

His eyes squint. "Why does that scare you, beautiful?" He pushes my hair away from my face, his fingertips skimming lightly across my cheek.

"I'm fucking broken. Don't you know that? If I let you in and you hurt me, I may not recover from that. I barely have a heart left after Katie. I can't lose any more of it." Tears sting my eyes and roll down my cheeks. I've been holding in too much lately. It's all been building and building and now, it's finally exploding.

"Shhh." He pulls me closer, cradling my head to his chest. "I'm not going to hurt you. I want to be with you. From the first time my eyes landed on yours—filled with pain and sadness—I wanted you. I wanted to be the one to make all that disappear. I know what broken looks like, and it's not you."

I look up into his blue eyes and see the pain hiding

beneath them. He wipes my tears away with his thumbs before moving in slowly for a kiss.

His hot mouth touches mine, and the floodgates open. A rush of emotion washes over me: excitement, fear, desire, maybe even love if I would let myself admit it. But I won't. Not yet. I can't.

He's kissing me softly but deeply. A kiss that sinks into me, reaching even the darkest, most broken parts of me. He's being so gentle, like he's afraid I will break. And I just might. Is this worth all the pain and suffering I'd have to go through? The touch of his skin, the feel of his kiss, the emotions he can stir inside of me, is it worth it?

He lies me back, covering my body with his, but he doesn't put his weight on me. He holds himself up so his hands can softly roam my body, sending shocks through me. His touch almost burns me, it's so strong and intense.

He breaks our kiss to pull my shirt from my body as he gets up on his knees, hovering over me.

"Do you even know how fucking sexy you were on that stage tonight?" He removes his shirt, tossing it onto the floor. "I wanted you so fucking bad." His fingers snake beneath my panties as he pulls them from my body. "I would have taken you right there on that stage with everyone watching if you'd let me." He pushes his pants down over his large erection and my stomach muscles tighten, needing him inside me, needing him to make me forget everything but the way I feel about him. "You had me so fucking worked up. I wanted to beat anyone who even looked at you." He slams into me, making me call out loudly. The bed moves with his powerful thrust, it hits the wall with a loud bang.

His hands are holding my hips, holding me still as I try to wiggle against him. I need him to move. Already my release is begging to be let free.

He pulls out slowly and pauses. "You're mine. And I'm yours. Say it."

"I'm yours," I practically moan, fisting my own hair, slightly pulling.

He pushes back into me, our skin slaps together as the headboard hits the wall again. "And?" he growls.

"You're mine!" I scream.

Finally, he pulls out suddenly and slams into me just as quick. But this time, he doesn't pause or slow. This time, he's lost control and he pumps into me hard and fast, unable to stop.

Before I know what is happening, he's rolling us over so I'm on top. "I want to watch you ride me." There is this rawness about him that makes my stomach clench while my arousal drenches him.

I begin moving up and down his length while watching him. I want to see what I do to him.

"You had me so fucking hard when you were up there with that *fuck me* look in your eyes. All I could think about was sinking myself deep inside that soaking wet pussy of yours."

His words do more to me than anything else. Knowing

that I teased him and had him so worked up makes my body hum, craving every inch of him. Just from thinking about how turned on I had him causes my orgasm to build inside of me. I call out while he thrusts up from beneath me. His hands squeeze my thighs as I grind against him, bringing me to the tip-top of my release before it shatters and rains down on me.

As I'm riding out every last wave, he quickly rolls me over and pumps into me until he's shattering right along with me.

He rolls to his back and pulls me against his chest. My hair clings to my sticky skin and I push it away before listening to the deep drum of his erratic heart.

"I am sorry for what I said earlier."

I feel his head move, trying to see me in the darkened room. "I'm sorry for making you jealous. I didn't mean to, but when I saw how cute you look when you're angry, I saw how it drove you to act the way you really wanted, without being held back, I couldn't help myself. You were free tonight. I saw all your insecurities fall away while you were up there throwing everything on the table."

I smile and roll to my stomach to see his face. "I think you owe me something now."

I can see the shadow his smile creates on his face. "What do you want to know?"

I think it over quickly. "Earlier when you told me about your friend. You seemed so full of regret. Like maybe if you had stayed there with him, he would still be here."

He doesn't reply, but I can feel his eyes on me. "The day you saw me at Katie's parents' house, did you see the same thing in me that you saw in him? Is that why we're together, because you were afraid to turn your back on me in fear I may hurt myself?"

He rolls us over and brushes my hair away from my eyes. "God no. I could have seen you on the street and had the same overwhelming feeling of need for you. I didn't want to save you. I just fucking wanted you. My soul wanted you. It's like you're my other half that I didn't realize I was missing until I saw you."

I nod as my eyes fill with tears. I know what he's talking about because it's the exact same way I feel about him. I don't know what this connection is, soulmates or two broken people finding some relief in each other, but whatever it is, it's strong and it doesn't waver. No matter how hard I tried to ignore it or run from it, it's still there, growing stronger with each passing moment we share together.

WE WAKE in the morning in a tangled mess. My left leg is thrown over his right leg. My right arm is under his pillow while his right arm is drooped over my side, holding me close.

He hasn't woke yet, so I hold real still and just allow myself a few minutes of admiration. If I look at him this way when he's awake, his head will swell and it's already big enough.

His beautiful blue eyes are closed and covered by long eyelashes any girl would kill for. His soft lips are slightly apart, blowing his warm breath across my face. This man is absolutely gorgeous, everything from his six pack abs, to his hard and toned biceps, to his jaw bones that go on for days. He looks like a Greek God, but with a dirtier, rougher edge to him.

His eyes flutter open and he offers a sleepy smile. "Why are you watching me sleep?"

"Because I'm awake and didn't want to wake you."

He untangles himself from me. "How are you even up? Aren't you hungover? I saw the way you sucked that fish bowl down last night."

Now that he mentions it I do feel like shit. My stomach churns and a dull ache ringing through my head makes itself known.

"Yeah, I'm never drinking again." I remember the last time I thought that exact same thing and it sends a jolt straight to my heart.

He sits up, grabbing something off the night stand before turning back to me. "A little hair of the dog?" He tosses me the flask.

I want to puke on him for even suggesting that. "Fuck no!" I toss it back as he chuckles and stands from the bed, completely naked. His toned back and firm ass tease me. I feel the pool gathering between my legs.

As he rounds the corner of the bed, his eyes fall on me and my heavy breathing. "See something you like, sweetheart?"

"I see a lot of things I like."

He motions towards the bathroom with his head. "Why don't you come join me and let me clean that dirty mind of yours?"

"I like it dirty."

He grins. "Oh, it won't stay clean long because I plan on dirtying it right back up as I fuck you from behind in that shower."

My heart leaps to my throat as I quickly stand and rush to the bathroom for all the dirty things promised.

WE SPENT ENTIRELY WAY TOO much time in the room, but it wasn't a waste. I enjoyed every, last, dirty minute of it. By the time we get back on the road, it's nearing two P.M, River insists on driving, saying my driving makes him nauseous. I don't argue because I have more fun watching him than the road.

We just get into Louisiana when I pull out my list and cross off the last thing I accomplished.

"If Katie were here, she probably wouldn't believe that I have done all this stuff."

River looks at me quickly before turning his attention

back to the road. "If she was still here, would you be doing that list?"

"Probably not. I had decided right after she wrote down '*kiss a stranger,*' that this list wouldn't get done."

"I'm glad you decided to go through with that one. The striptease though…"

I take a sudden breath as I turn to look at him. "What? I thought you liked it?"

He nods once. "I did like it. But there was nothing on there that said it had to be public. I bet I would've liked it just as much, if not better, if it was just the two of us."

"Well, someone once told me that if I was going to do this list, I needed to do it right," I taunt him with his own words.

He rolls his eyes. "I'm not always right, you know."

"Whoa, slow down a minute! Can I get a video of you admitting that?"

He laughs out loud before pulling me over to him for a quick kiss. "Not on your life."

Our conversation flows easy as we speed down the highway with nothing to hold us back. All the stress from the day before is long gone and forgotten about. I'm not trying to hold myself back anymore. When I took this challenge, it was to free myself and everything that came along with it. River and the things I feel for him are one of those things. I may end up with a broken heart, but I know now that it is most definitely worth it.

WE TAKE our time getting to Florida. The journey is half the fun. We stay up making love as long as we can, and then we sleep late, not getting up until we have had at least an hour of cuddling, kissing, and touching.

I managed to find us a small, one bedroom apartment to rent for the summer, and it's on its own private beach. I had to do some convincing with the building manager, but I managed to get us in, and I even have a plan to get River back for the walk of shame I had to do at the tent.

We pull into the parking lot around two P.M. I step out and look up. The apartments almost look like a row of houses. They are all connected, but each is set up as its own place, having its own front door, back door, and roof. I retrieve the key and pay the bill for the summer, before showing River in.

The hardwood floors shine beneath our feet as we walk through. The living room is decent, home to only a small, blue couch, a little TV, and a couple of end tables with matching lamps. I move further, reaching the kitchen and breakfast nook. There is a sliding glass door that leads directly to the beach. Time to put my plan into action.

I spin around to face River. "Are you excited?"

He smiles as he closes the distance between us. His lips quickly smack against mine. "Let's celebrate." He starts pulling me in the direction that leads to the bathroom and bedroom.

I hold up my finger. "Okay, but first, there is one thing I didn't tell you about this place because I wanted to surprise you."

"What is it?" His blue eyes are gleaming.

"The beach we're on…"

"Mm-hmm," he says against the soft skin of my neck.

"It's a private nude beach."

He pulls away suddenly. "Are you serious?"

I laugh and nod. "Want to go for a naked swim?"

"Hell yeah!" He pulls his shirt above his head. His shoes, socks, jeans, and boxers follow quickly after.

I pull my shirt off and toss it on top of his clothes. "Oh, go ahead. I'm going to grab us some towels and I'll catch up to you."

"Alright." He presses one last kiss to my lips before unlocking the door and sliding it open.

A wide smile covers my face as I turn around and cross my arms over my chest, waiting.

"Five."

"Four."

"Three."

"Two."

"On— "

River rushes back into the room. He closes the door quickly behind him and pulls the curtain closed. He spins around and presses his back to the glass like he can't even stand anymore.

"What's the matter?" I smile.

His eyes are wide and his face is slightly pale, almost green. "You…you did that on purpose."

"Did what?" I move towards him and try pushing him out of the way to look out. I know what I'll see. "I promise it is a nude beach, was everyone else wearing suits?" I feign innocence.

He turns around to stop me from opening the curtain. "No. This is a retirement home, isn't it?"

I bust out laughing. "It's assisted living!"

His hands fly to his hair, making it stand in all directions. "It was horrible. I've never seen so many saggy, wrinkly breasts in my whole life."

I fall into the floor, holding my stomach from laughing so hard.

"Balls swinging between two little, boney knees." His voice is filled with disgust and fear, and it only makes me laugh harder.

My eyes are leaking tears faster than I can wipe them away, and my lungs burn for oxygen.

"It's not funny. One old man dropped his sunglasses. He bent down and I *saw* things…" his words are cut off by a loud gagging sound.

"Stop! Please stop!" I say around a fit of laughter. "I can't—I can't take anymore." I'm shaking my head, unable to move from the floor.

Suddenly, River looks pissed, but even that doesn't stop the tickle in my stomach from getting him back.

"Why'd you do that? You had to know this is a nursing

home and not regular apartments. How'd you even get us in here?"

I hold out my hand for him to help me up as my laughing dies down. "I didn't get this place to burn you, but I had to take the opportunity. I know how you hate missing out on once in a lifetime chances." Another bout of laughter escapes me.

"Jovi?"

Oh my God! I have to stop laughing. Think of something sad.

Katie.

My laughing slows, allowing me to wipe the tears away from my eyes, and I take a deep breath.

I look at River standing in front of me with his hands on his naked hips, eyes trained on me.

"They had a vacancy. After I promised we wouldn't have any parties, that they didn't have to feed us with the rest of the occupants, and I would pay for all three months up front, they wavered. I didn't know about the private nude beach until after the place was reserved."

"What did I do to you to make you hate me this much?" His face is now showing a bit of amusement, but his skin color is still slightly off.

"The wet and wild walk of shame!"

His head falls back, looking at the ceiling, as a grin takes over his face. "I didn't do that on purpose," he proclaims.

"Yeah, well now we're even." I poke his chest as I move

in to hug him. He starts pulling off my bra and unbuttoning my pants.

"What are you doing?" I ask around my smile.

"I need to see you naked now. That…" he uses his hand to motion toward the beach. "…cannot be the last thing these eyes have seen. I'll have nightmares."

I laugh but allow him to pull off my clothes. We're both totally naked, holding onto one another in the breakfast room when he leans in, pressing a kiss to my lips. When he pulls away, his smile is back in place. "That was a good burn. But I'm afraid you've started something here."

I step away. "Oh no! I wasn't trying to start something, I was trying to end it."

"I didn't do that on purpose!" He points at me as I begin to pull away.

"Whatever." I reach around his neck and direct his lips back to mine.

He breaks the kiss for just a second. "It's on!"

AFTER WE TAKE our time enjoying what will be our little home for the next three months, we decide to go check out our surroundings. The place we're in has its own spa, casino, and restaurant, along with different community rooms where dances and games are held.

I take River's hand and lead him out the door and across the parking lot towards the main building.

"Are you serious about this?" he complains, dragging his feet.

"It may be fun. Let's just check it out."

He grumbles something I don't catch, but keeps moving.

I scan the keycard I was given to get into the main building and open the door. This is like a little town for the retired. The main building has small shops and stores, restaurants, a gym and spa, and even a grocery store. A little golf cart drives along the property, picking up the residents and bringing them to the main building so they can hang out with friends or do some shopping. I don't know why my grandma had such a fit when she was placed in one of these places. This looks fun to me!

I lead us into the casino and walk up to the window.

"Can I help you?" the lady behind the desk asks.

"We're staying here for the summer and we were just checking the place out. How does all of this work?"

She seems a little confused, probably because I'm not a retiring senior. "Most of our occupants have money put into their account by their families. They are given a set limit on what they can spend a month, but the machines don't pay out any money like a regular casino. What they win is credited to their account which they can spend here or in any of the shops on the property."

"Oh." I feel my face redden. Of course this isn't like a regular casino. I'm about to tell her thank you and walk away when I hear a commotion behind me.

I turn around to see a group of old ladies circling around

River. "You're that young man from the beach, aren't you? I'd recognize that nice rear end anywhere," one lady says. And based on how high River jumps, I'm guessing she pinched his 'nice rear end'.

I can't help the wide smile that spreads across my face. But he doesn't look entertained. He's giving me the death glare with the ladies flocking around him.

"Come by my room later, sugar. I'll teach you how to play pinochle," the lady with a gray wig tells him.

I double over, laughing.

"That's very nice of you ladies, but I really need to go and…I just need to go." He squeezes between them because they are not backing away to let him leave.

He grabs my arm. "I'm sooo getting you back." He drags me from the room, while my giggles continue.

As we're walking down the hall towards the exit, another lady approaches us. River stops, being the polite man he is, but he doesn't look happy about it.

"Hi there, sweet-stuff. I saw you on the beach today and couldn't help but to notice how thin you are. So I whipped up a batch of brownies." She smiles at him sweetly before giving me the death glare. "Don't you know how to feed your man?" she asks me.

My mouth hangs open. What happened to sweet old ladies? The only ones I've seen here are horny as hell.

River takes the plate and bows his head. "Thank you. That's very nice of you, Mrs…"

She turns back to him, sweetness dripping from her voice as she says, "Ms. Pen. Vivian Pen."

River holds out his hand and she places hers in his. He places a kiss to the top. "It was a pleasure to meet you, Ms. Pen. And thank you for the brownies. I won't be sharing any of them." He flashes me an annoyed look.

I roll my eyes and cross my arms over my chest.

The lady blushes and covers her smile with her hand.

Before anyone can say anything else, River grabs my wrist again and pulls me out the door.

"You're sooo dead," he seethes.

"Please, stop. My stomach can't handle any more laughing." I hold my side that is already aching.

12

Truth or Dare

River refuses to leave the room for the rest of the day. He snacks on his brownies that look thick and delicious, but he refuses to give me one. We watch some TV and finally break out his flask because we're both so bored. I wanted to go to Miami Beach, but it was already so late in the day that I decided to push it off until tomorrow.

I pull out my list as we're sitting on the floor around the coffee table, taking turns with the flask. I make sure I've marked off everything that I can, and study it for my next accomplishment.

"Hey, I know what we can do."

"What's that?" His eyes find mine.

"We can play truth or dare." I flip the notebook around to show him number nineteen.

His brow wrinkles. "How have you gone your whole life and not played truth or dare?"

I set the list back down on the table. "I was always afraid I'd have to do or answer something embarrassing, so I never played."

He shakes his head but agrees.

"Okay, truth or dare?" I ask him.

"Truth."

I think up a question. I don't want to get into anything too hard or deep just yet. I want to play nice so that maybe he will do the same with me. "What's your last name?" I can't believe I never thought to ask him that before.

"Wilce," he answers.

"Hmmm. River Wilce." *Jovi Wilce?* That sounds weird but I bet I could get used to it.

"Truth or dare?" he asks me.

I think it over, going with the 'ease into it' approach. "Truth."

He places his hand on the floor behind him and leans back while watching me. "Did you enjoy being on that stage, stripping while all eyes were on you?"

My heart picks up, and my stomach fills with butterflies at the memory. I swallow down my fear with another shot. "I did. It was exhilarating, not that it is something I will ever do again."

He smiles like he knew he was right the whole time.

"Truth or dare?"

"Dare," he says, eyes darkening.

"I dare you to remove all your clothes…"

"Hell yeah!" He stands.

"Wait, I'm not done. I dare you to remove all your clothes and wear them backwards for the rest of the day."

He scoffs. "Fine, that's easy." He pulls off his shirt and turns it around backwards. I stand to button up the back of it.

"Truth or dare?" he asks as he removes his boxers and jeans and spins them around.

I move around to the back of him and zip and button his jeans before fixing his belt. "Dare." It only seems fair at this point. And as soon as I can get this out of the way, I can be done with the game and cross it off my list.

River faces me with an evil smile. "I dare you to strip and walk out that door for a swim. Then walk back."

"What? No way, there are people still out there. The sun hasn't even gone down yet!"

He laughs. "It's a dare. You have to."

Fuck. I take a deep breath before letting it out slowly. I turn for the door and stare out it while removing my clothes. River leans against the wall, snacking on another brownie as he watches.

Once I'm completely naked, I slide the door open and step out onto the warm sand. As I walk slowly across the beach, all the old men freeze and watch me. I turn to see River standing in the same spot, eating his brownie with a huge smile on his face.

"I hate you," I mouth at him. I turn around and finish

my journey to the water. I walk in until I'm deep enough, and dive under. I swim in a big circle and come out. As I'm starting my walk back, I realize that this only makes it look even more erotic since I'm soaking wet with water rolling down all my curves.

Every old man on the beach is frozen, all but their eyes that are following me. All the ladies at their sides are yelling at their men and slapping their arms to stop them from looking at me.

I rush back inside the door and smack him on the arm. "I hate you."

He pulls me against his chest. "No you don't." His lips land on mine and, before I know what's happening, he has my naked body lying back on the table while he's driving deep inside me.

It's hard, fast, and full of passion, but it doesn't last long.

He holds out his hand and I take it in mine as he pulls me to my feet. "What got into you?" I ask with a smile.

He shakes his head. "I don't know. I feel funny."

I draw my brows together. "What do you mean? Are you getting sick?" I ask as I start pulling my clothes back on.

"No, nothing like that," he says with his back to me.

"Well what's the matter?" I latch onto his arm and spin him around. He's completely naked, cupping his junk with his hands.

I look at the place his hands are hiding and then back up to his eyes. "Are— are you hard again?"

His Adam's apple bobs as he nods, a little unsure of what is happening to his body.

Suddenly, I put two and two together. "I'll be right back."

"Wait! Where are you going? I need you," he pouts.

"Two minutes," I promise before rushing out the door.

I make the quick walk back to the main building and search through the casino, shops, and finally the game room. My eyes land on Ms. Pen and I rush to her side.

"Okay, old lady. What did you put in the brownies?" I put my hand on my hip.

She looks at me, taken back. "The same thing I put in all the brownies for the men around here. There's cocoa powder, eggs, flour…"

"Cut the shit. What's the *special* ingredient?"

"Just these little blue pills that the men pop like candy. Why? What's the big deal?"

I burst out laughing, knowing exactly what little blue pill she's talking about.

I rush back to the room to find River in the bathroom. I knock on the door. "Riv? Are you okay?"

I can hear his heavy breathing through the door.

"Are you taking care of your little problem?"

I hear the toilet flush before the water comes on. A few seconds later, he's opening the door, his dick tenting his boxers. "Three times I've taken care of my "little" problem. It won't go the fuck away. What's going on?"

I get way too much pleasure telling him this. "Ms. Pen added a secret ingredient that all the men around here like."

He shakes his head with a raise of his brows. "Which is?"

"Viagra!" I can't hold back the laughter anymore. It's completely taken over.

"Fuck! Are you serious?"

I nod while covering my mouth.

"It's not funny, Jovi. It really hurts."

His confession only makes it worse for me.

He flexes his jaw as he leans against the wall, not looking at me, but straight ahead. "Are you done?"

I hold up my finger and let out one more, loud round of laughter.

Finally when I have managed to calm myself down, I dry my face of all the tears. "Okay, what can we do?" I ask, still out of breath.

"I don't know!" He's pacing back and forth across the floor now.

"Ice! We'll get you some ice." I rush to the fridge and pull out an ice tray, emptying it into a bag.

He moves to sit on the couch, and I hand him the bag that he places on his crotch.

I sit down beside him and we both blankly stare at the TV. I turn to him. "So, three times?"

"Three fucking times! And that was *after* we had sex!"

"How many brownies did you eat?"

He breathes deep. "The whole plate."

I turn my head away from him and cover my mouth to laugh.

"Ha ha ha," he mocks bitterly, only making me laugh harder.

"IT SAYS HERE if you have an erection for four hours to seek medical attention. How long has it been?"

"Six hours," he answers flatly.

I stand. "Let's go."

His eyes flash to mine, his eyebrows are drawn together, and his jaw is flexed with tension. "I can't go out like *this*." He lifts the bag of nothing but water now, showing me the tent in his boxers.

"If you like your little man you better. It says an erection lasting over four hours can *permanently* damage the penis."

"What do you mean little? Look at this thing!" He raises his eyebrows indignantly.

I stifle back my laugh, knowing it will only anger him more. "Oh, I got an idea." I rush around and grab my bag. I dig until I come up with a thin scarf. "Pull your boxers down."

He rolls his eyes but pulls them down. I wrap the scarf around his thigh. "Okay, push it down against your leg."

He does so and I wrap the scarf around it, tying it down. It tries to spring back up, but the scarf holds it in place. "There, now get your clothes on and let's go."

"I can't stand up straight."

"Why not?" I question.

"You try having your dick tied to your leg and see if you can stand up straight!"

I snicker but nod with understanding. "Okay, I'll help you, sit down."

He sits down and I grab his jeans and sit on the floor at his feet. "Slide your feet in."

"You have them backwards."

I look up at him. "A dare is a dare!"

His nostrils flair and he grounds his teeth together, but he allows me to put them on backwards.

I grab my purse and hold onto his arm, leading him to the car.

We get to the hospital a short while later and River tries turning around the second we're inside and at the desk.

"What's going on with you today?" the lady behind the glass asks as she takes in his backwards clothes.

"Umm." He looks from me to her and then back. "Nothing. I'm fine." He tries to turn again, but I grab hold of his arm and keep him in place.

"He accidentally ingested Viagra, and he's had a litt— I mean, big problem for the last six hours." I look over at River. "See, I didn't say little *this* time." I smile up at him as I nudge him with my elbow.

The lady behind the glass nods with wide eyes. "I see." She slides us a clipboard of papers. "Please fill this out. The doctor will be with you soon."

We don't wait long before a doctor walks in and calls River's name. We both stand but he stops and looks at me.

"Oh, do you want me to wait here?"

He offers up a sarcastic smile. "Yeah, it would be great if I didn't have to listen to you laugh the whole time."

"Completely understandable." I sit back down and watch him walk away with the doctor.

A couple of hours later, River comes walking out. He's standing up right, head held high and shoulders squared. "Let's go."

I grab my bag and rush behind him.

When we get into the car, I slide behind the wheel and start the engine. "So? What'd they say? What'd they do?"

He doesn't look at me. He keeps his eyes straight ahead. "They had to drain it." His hands are covering his groin.

I shift into drive. "Drain it? Like, with a needle?"

He doesn't move his head, but he looks at me from the corner of his eye, confirming my guess.

I hold my breath to keep my laughter inside but it's threatening to come out. I put the car back into park, turn my head toward the window, and cover my face with my hand. I'm trying so hard to keep it in, but a snort comes out, followed by a screeching sound.

He doesn't say anything or move. He just waits for it to pass.

WHEN WE GET BACK to the apartment, he doesn't waste any time. He pulls off his backward clothes and falls into bed. I lean against the doorframe, watching him. He looks so innocent in his sleep. I pull off my clothes and join him. He wraps his arm around me in his sleep, and pulls me closer. His heat settles over me thicker than a blanket, and it soothes me into a deep dreamless sleep.

I WAKE the next morning and River is still sound asleep. He must have had a traumatic day yesterday.

I get up without waking him and slip into the shower.

When I step out, I set to work on making breakfast for him. I feel bad for laughing at him so much yesterday, but I couldn't control it. I realize now how dangerous the situation could have been. I shake my head when I think about how this whole thing started: a few guys seeing me naked at the campsite. Hell, a fish bowl drink and a day later, their show could have been a lot better.

My face heats up with those thoughts. That night, the one with the strip show, it's getting filed into my 'do not remember' closet in my brain. It's like the rules of Vegas. What happened that night, stays with that night.

I push the embarrassing thoughts from my head and scramble some eggs. I'm dancing and singing along with

Tighten Up by The Black Keys when I hear a quiet tapping sound. I crane my neck to see River still passed out in bed. I move to the front door and open it to find plates with homemade goodies on the doorstep. There is even a fruit basket and flowers.

I laugh to myself but pick up the treats. I'm not sure if this is a sweet gesture or not, considering we didn't get anything until we got naked.

I unload the arm full of treats onto the counter just as River walks into the room. "What's all this stuff?" He uses his head to motion toward the gifts.

"Things our admirers left out on our front step. Are you hungry for some homemade cookies this time?" I tease him.

He picks up everything that's not factory sealed and throws it in the trash. "What the hell? Since when is it okay to drug people?" He runs his hand through his blond hair, leaving it spiking in all directions.

I shrug. "If it makes you feel better, I don't think that lady knew what the pills did. She just knew all the old men around here liked them."

"It doesn't make me feel better. It makes me feel dirty. It's like she was hoping for that reaction and for my dick to lead me to her."

I scoff. "Don't be dramatic. Her hip couldn't handle you." I reach out and pinch his nipple.

He jumps and backs away. "Don't do that."

"Do what?" I ask with a smile as I step closer, reaching for anything I can grab.

"I don't want to be touched while we're talking about those dirty ladies." He visibly shivers.

I let out a loud laugh. "How's the big man in your pants feeling today, anyway?" I move back to the stove and scoop some eggs onto two plates for us.

"A little sore. Like he ran a marathon all night." He cups his hand over his crotch.

I nod towards the couch. "Come on. Let's take it easy before we head out for the day."

13

Join me on the beach

AFTER WE EAT BREAKFAST, I PULL ON MY 'BARELY THERE' bikini with some shorts and a tank top and we head to the beach, the beach that Katie should be lounging on, sipping cocktails right now. On the drive there, I grasp the charm on my necklace, the only piece of her that I have left.

Even though River had such a tough day yesterday, he's doing everything he can to be here for me like he knows how hard this is going to be. He fills his flask full and hands it over to me to slip into the beach bag.

As we walk closer to the sand, his hand finds mine. He squeezes it slightly, trying to offer me support and comfort.

Just walking across the soft sand makes my eyes tear. My chest tightens from trying to hold them back, and my heart that I thought was already shattered grinds down to a fine dust, almost like the sand under my feet.

I step under the cabana I rented and pull off my clothes before relaxing in a lounge chair. I can feel River's eyes on me, but I don't look at him. I'm not sure if he's checking me out because of my bikini, or if it's because he's afraid finally being here with Katie gone is going to destroy me.

I see a waiter walk by and I call out to him. He walks over and I look him up and down. He's wearing a pair of white board shorts that hug his hips. Every muscle in his body is ripped and covered in tan skin. I'm sure Katie would approve. However, I wonder which she would choose when it came to River: screw, kill, or marry?

I snap out of my thoughts before ordering two mixed drinks.

"Why did you order two? Are you *that* thirsty today?" River asks curiously from beside me.

I shake my head while staring out over the water. "No, one is for Katie." I pull the list out of the bag and open it to the last page. The very last thing she wrote was *"join me on the beach for a drink"*. She was determined to get me here one way or another, and she succeeded.

I cross through it as a tear slides down my cheek. It drips from my chin and lands on the paper, smearing the ink. "I'm here, Katie. Now what?"

The waiter returns and hands me one drink while he places the other on the table between River and I. I sip the fruity mixture and it cools me off. I know Katie wouldn't want me to be sad, but I can't help feel lonely here without her. I miss her.

This is something we should have done together. More tears build in my eyes and I don't bother hiding them. They need to fall. I need them out. I didn't think this would be as difficult as it is. I also expected to feel a little closer to her, like this would be some kind of connection for us. But sitting here now without her, she couldn't feel any further away.

I wipe my tears away and notice River is reaching out his hand. I take it in mine and our eyes meet. "I know this is going to be hard on you, but I just want to let you know I'm here. If you need to cry or scream or hit something, I'm here." He looks so sincere it makes my heart swell.

I nod and dry my face as I pick up my glass and drink it quicker than necessary.

The frozen drink helps to keep me cool while the heat of the day and the bright sun warm my skin. A slight breeze blows through the thin material of the cabana and it relaxes me. I allow my eyes to close as I hold the charm on my necklace in my fist.

"HEY. WAKE UP, LAZY ASS," Katie says as she shakes my arm.

My eyes flutter open and I sit up quickly, looking around

me. I'm still in my beach chair, only it isn't River sitting beside me, it's Katie.

"What are you doing here? You're- you're gone," I cry.

Her bottom lip comes out in a pout. "I know. I'm sorry I had to leave you."

I swing my legs over the side of the chair to face her directly. "Why did this happen? I can't do this without you."

"You can do this, Jo. You have been doing it. Look at all the things you've done since I've been gone."

"I only did those things for the list you made. I felt like I owed it to you." I know this is a dream, but I can't stand to look away from her in fear I will wake up and never seen her again. A dream of her is better than nothing.

She smiles brightly with her blonde curls blowing in the gentle breeze. "I know why you did them, but you still did them. By the time you finish that list, you won't need me anymore."

I shake my head, tears now welling up in my eyes. "I'll always need you. I have no idea what I'm doing."

"Yes, you do." She nods, assuring me. "You have everything covered." Her eyes are wide and shining brightly as she stands from her chair and sits down beside me. She wraps her arm around my shoulders and pulls me in for a hug. I can feel it like she's really here with me. "You'll even get a little surprise by the time that list is done. Trust me. Trust in yourself." She hugs me and presses a kiss to my forehead before standing. "I love you, Jo," she says with a smile as she stands to walk away from me.

"I love you, Katie." I whisper the words, but it's like she can hear them anyway because she looks over her shoulder at me.

"Don't catch any diseases," I call after her.

She lifts her middle finger and flips me off, like I knew she would, before disappearing from view.

MY EYES FLUTTER open to see River watching me.

"Why are you smiling?" he asks me.

I sit upright and pick up his flask. "I had a dream about Katie." I reach down and see that I'm still clutching the charm in my other hand.

I know that was nothing more than a simple dream, my subconscious trying to give me something I desperately want, but it feels like more. It feels like she was actually here with me. I can still smell her perfume. I can still feel her arm around me.

More tears sting my eyes. She's my best friend, and she's gone. I don't know if this spot inside of me will ever heal, or if I'll ever learn to live without her.

RIVER and I spend the rest of the day at the beach. We move our chairs closer together so we can hold hands while we soak up the sun and the heat. I sip on mixed drinks and his flask, trying to come to terms with how I will have to live my life from now on.

I try distracting myself with River and his sculpted body lying next to mine. I feel myself blush when he sees me checking him out.

"Stop that."

"Stop what?" I ask, surprised.

"I'm out of commission for a few days. And the way you're looking at me, I won't be able to keep my hands to myself. No boners for a week."

"A *week*?" I ask, my voice raising to an unnatural pitch.

He lets out a deep chuckle. "What's the matter, princess? Can't go that long without me?"

I turn my head and close my eyes to let the sun warm my face. "I guess I'll just have to pick up the slack for you."

He groans. "Don't even say that. Just thinking about you touching yourself will give me a hard on."

I smile, happy with torturing him.

When the sun starts to set, we pack up and go back to the car to head home for the day. River drives because I've drank all day. He didn't drink a drop. I think it was his way of telling me to just relax for the day.

I keep his flask in my hand as we drive down the road. I uncap it and go to take a drink when the cap falls from my fingers, rolling under the seat. "Fuck." I bend down and feel under the seat, but don't feel it.

I pull my knees up and flip around with my head in the

floorboard to look under the seat. I feel the car swerve and then hear police sirens.

I pop up quickly. "What's going on?"

"Fuck! We're being pulled over. You had to have your ass in the air, didn't you?" He's frowning while his eyes flash from the road to the rearview mirror.

"How did my ass get us pulled over?" My voice is high pitched and loud from being blamed for this.

"I can't touch you, I had to look," he says as he pulls the car to the shoulder of the road.

I want to laugh at his confession, but the seriousness of it all is muffling my amusement.

The cop taps on the window and River rolls his down.

"Do you know why I pulled you over?" he asks.

River doesn't answer, just shrugs.

"You were speeding and driving erratically. I need your driver's license and registration."

"I don't have it on me," River answers.

I feel my mouth hang open. *How do you not have your license on you?*

"What's your name and date of birth? I'll look you up?"

River's head leans back against the seat. "I'll just save you some time, I don't have a license."

"How do you not have a license?" I yell, unable to hold it in. He's been doing most of the fucking driving and he doesn't have a license?

His head jerks in my direction. "I just moved from New York City. Nobody has a license!"

"Ma'am, is that alcohol?" the police officer asks.

I suddenly realize I'm still holding the open flask in my hand. "No!" I quickly answer.

He motions for the flask, but I hold it out the window, quickly pouring it out on the ground.

The police officer rushes around the car and grabs the flask from my hand. He raises it to his nose. "You know drinking in a motor vehicle is against the law, right?"

I bat my eyes at him and smile. "I had no idea."

"Step out of the car ma'am." He opens my door.

"Hey, wait just a minute," River says, getting out of the car and rushing around to my side.

The cop, feeling danger, spins River around and presses him against the car. River thrashes against him, trying to explain, but the officer slaps cuffs on him and walks him back to the police car.

"I'm afraid you're going in too," he says while motioning for me to step out of the car. He allows me to step out on my own and I put my hands behind my back as he puts the cuffs in place.

"Can you grab my purse for me?" I ask nicely.

He takes my purse and puts it in the front seat of the police car before placing me in the backseat next to River.

He stands outside the car, talking on his radio.

"I can't believe you don't have a license!" I yell at River.

"I can't believe you poured out my flask! Do you know how expensive that scotch was?" He rolls his eyes.

I shake my head, unable to believe this is where our day is heading. We're being arrested and all he's worried about is his scotch.

"At least we're in the right place to keep you from popping a boner," I say from inside the jail cell.

"You're so not funny." He lifts his head from the wall to give me a dirty look.

"Hey, this is all your fault. You shouldn't drive without a license."

"And you shouldn't drink in a car, have your ass up in the air, or pour out good booze." He lists them off on his fingers.

"Jovi?" an officer asks, walking by the cell.

I jump up. "Yes! That's me!"

"You've made bail. Payment just came through." He opens the cell, allowing me to step out. River stands. "What about me?"

"I'll bail you out, babe. But it'll cost ya," I tease with him, still feeling my buzz.

He rolls his eyes before running his hand through his hair. "Never mind. I'll hang here." He sits back down.

I laugh and blow him a kiss before walking away with the police officer.

After my belongings have been returned, I pay the one-hundred and fifty dollars to bail River out.

It takes them almost an hour to process him, but finally, we're able to leave with a promise to appear in court in a few months.

The first thing we do is head over to the impound lot and bail the car out of jail. By the time we get home, we're both so exhausted, we go right to bed, too tired to even think of trying to cross off anything else on the list.

I'm LOUNGING across my bed, doing homework and listening to music when Katie bursts into my room. She looks pissed as hell as she slams the door behind her and paces the floor.

I pull my earbuds out and drop them onto the bed as I sit up, watching her. "What's going on?"

She spins around to face me. "I think my parents are going to get a divorce."

"What? Why?"

She walks across the room and sits down beside me. "Do you remember last year when my dad came home and him and my mom got into a fight in the kitchen?"

I nod.

"Well, things have been strained since then. They're hardly ever in the same room. When they are, they don't talk, and sometimes at night, I hear them fighting. They never used to fight before that day."

"So what are they fighting about?" I ask, pulling my legs up underneath me.

"I don't know. All I can get is that a man named Josh showed up, asking for money."

"Who is Josh, and why would he show up asking for money?"

She shrugs while picking at the skin around her fingernails. "I don't know. But my dad wants to give him the money, and my mom doesn't. I heard her say that my dad made his choice, and he can't take it back now."

"Then what happened?" I ask her.

"He stormed out of their bedroom and left. I tried to sit up and wait for him to come home, but I fell asleep before he made it back."

I wrap my arm around her shoulders. "I'm sure everything will be fine, Katie. You're parents are just going through something. They'll work it out."

"I hope you're right."

I'M SITTING on the couch with my list when River walks in.

"What are you doing?" He plops down beside me.

"I just marked off *'get arrested'* from the list. So what do I want to know about you now?" I tap my finger on my chin.

"Ask away." He lies back on the couch, propping his head up on the arm, looking at me.

"I don't know what else to ask you. Just tell me something."

He shakes his head. "Nope. You have to ask the questions."

"I don't know what to ask. Tell me something that nobody else knows about you."

His blue eyes glaze over. "I'm in love with you."

I quickly turn my head away, starting at the floor on the other side of the room. I don't want to leave him hanging, but I'm not there yet. I can't say those words. I haven't even let myself admit how I feel about him yet. I was hoping to have this conversation at the end of the summer, when we get back home. I feel the couch move as he sits up.

"Jovi," he says almost in a whisper.

I don't answer him. I'm lost in my endless thoughts.

"Jovi." He places his hand under my chin and tilts my head in his direction so I have to look at him.

"I didn't say it to make you say it back. I know this summer is about finding yourself, and I'm not trying to confuse you. I just wanted you to know. I loved you the second you looked up at me with those big, brown, puppy dog eyes of yours." His lips move to mine. They are so soft and moving slow. He's trying to tell me something with this kiss, but what?

Is he trying to make me believe his words? Is he trying to make me forget that he said them because of my reaction?

I don't know, so I do the only thing I know how. I kiss him back. Feeling everything he has to give me, but refusing to search inside myself to see what I truly feel for him. I'm still too broken for that.

I turn and crawl up his body until I'm straddling him. His hands land on my hips as he squeezes them. He pulls away. "I can't do this yet."

I feel let down, but I *knew* this. He's hurt. I'm sure having a needle shoved in that part of your body will leave some lasting effects.

"I know. I just wanted to feel close to you. Give you something since I'm not quite ready to give you those words yet."

His Adam's apple bobs in his throat as his eyes darken. He stands with me in his arms, I squeal from the sudden movement. I hold on around his neck until I feel my back hit the bed with him standing over me. "What are you doing?"

His fingers slide into the waistband of my shorts as he pushes them down my legs. "Just because I can't, doesn't mean you can't.

He leans down, putting his mouth on me. His tongue runs between my folds and circles around my hard nub. Every once in a while, his wet tongue flicks over it, causing a surge of lightening to jolt through me.

He teases me with his mouth for what feels like hours. When I feel myself building, he changes pace, letting it slip away only to repeat the process of pushing me to the edge, just to pull me back.

I'm moaning and whimpering, pleading for my release,

but he doesn't relent. I'm dripping with need, I can no longer control the way my hips are moving, trying to get more of him.

His hands latch on to my hips, stopping my movements as he continues with his torture.

I try sliding my hands down to my sex to release my orgasm myself, and he pushes them away, holding them at my sides. "Not until I say." His voice is thick and full of desire.

He keeps pace, teasing me without release, finally he pulls away and I whimper, missing his touch. "Fuck it." He pulls his jeans down and crawls up my body. I don't refuse even though I should to keep him from hurting himself. His dick is practically throbbing while it stands at attention. He places himself at my entrance and pushes forward, gently.

He lets out a deep throaty sound just from being inside me. "You feel so good wrapped around me, Jovi."

My release is building even though he isn't moving. "River, please move. I'm about to come already."

His lips crash with mine as he gently slides out and softly pushes back in. His movements are so soft compared to how it usually feels. But my body doesn't care. It will take what it can get. My toes curl as my muscles tighten. Just as my orgasm rises again, he thrusts inside of me and fills me while I break around him.

His mouth is open with his eyes closed as he comes down from his high. He looks completely fucking erotic and it makes me want more of him, but I'm afraid of hurting him.

"How's he doing down there?"

He slides out of me and falls to my side. "Never better."

"It didn't hurt?"

"Fuck no. It felt too good to even last." He pulls me against him. "I've missed you." His hand travels from my navel down to the wet junction between my legs. "I don't think you're ready to stop yet." His fingers slide between my lips.

"I'm okay, I don't want to hurt you."

"I promise you can't hurt me." His breath blows across my skin as his fingers move quicker, bringing my orgasm to the surface again.

14
Is this the end?

As the summer goes by, River and I only get closer. And with each passing day, I'm that much closer to admitting how I feel about him. I still haven't let myself say the words, but they are on my tongue, waiting to break free.

We only have a week left here in Miami before we have to start our journey back to California. We've managed to mark almost everything off the list including, get a haircut I'd never get. My hair that has always hung to my waist has now been lopped off to my shoulders. I thought I was going to cry when she was cutting it, but by the end of it, I was in love. It's smooth and sleek now, and doesn't require a small army to tame and keep in place.

Katie was right about one thing, this has been the best summer of my life, other than losing her.

I've kept in contact with my parents. I talk to them most days, and my mom has been making sure my rent is paid so I still have an apartment when I get home. She doesn't know anything about River though. I had a feeling she would freak out if she found out I was traveling across the country with a guy I didn't know.

River has promised me a special night tonight and I'm a little nervous because I have no idea what he has in store. Every day with him is special, but he promised me it's something I won't ever forget.

I'm sitting in the kitchen, writing another letter to Katie when he walks in. I close the notebook that's nearly full now with letters to her.

"Are you ready?"

"Already? I didn't think we were going until later?" I replace the cap on my pen before standing.

"Nope. This is check off day!" He pulls me against his chest.

"What's check off day?" I look up at him and see a gleam reflecting in his eyes.

"The day we check everything else off that list, all in one day." He looks completely carefree and happy. It warms every part of me.

"Seriously? You think we can do the rest all in one day?"

"If we hurry." He takes my hand and pulls me towards the door.

"Where are we going first?" I ask him as I drive down the road.

"Turn here," he directs, pointing right.

I turn and follow along with his directions until he tells me to stop at a house. "Where are we?"

"I just met this guy. His name is Dave. Anyway, he's having a house party and guess what he has."

I feel my face wrinkle up as I look at the run down house with the grass growing up and trash overflowing from the garbage can that's still on the curb. There are used tires stacked up at the corner of his garage, bikes leaning against the front of the house, and a porch that seems to be a catch all for anything he can't fit inside his house. "A hoarding problem?"

He laughs. "No, a keg. You can do your keg stand."

"Oh, great," I say not all that excited about a keg stand. Compared to the other things I have checked off, this one is boring.

River leads me to the door and knocks before a big man wearing a white tank top answers. He's completely covered in tattoos, even his bald head. He reaches out his hand. "River! Glad to see ya bro." The guys shake hands. "And I'm glad you got your girl to come with you." He opens the door and lets us in.

"River told me all about your bucket list and I think it's great," he says as he leads us through the dirty house and out to the back yard.

"Here is it." Dave motions toward the keg. "Mark it off. Get your pretty ass up there."

I feel my face flush. "I have no idea how to do this."

"Don't worry about it. We'll help you out." He gets behind me and pushes me a couple steps closer. "Put each hand on the side of the keg," he directs.

I'm nervous but do as he tells me.

"River is going to get one leg and I'm going to get the other. The only thing you have to remember is to keep your arms locked. You don't want to land on your face."

"What?" I ask just as the guys lift my legs up. I scream, but before I know it, I'm upside down.

"Are you ready, babe?" River ask me as he raises the tap to my mouth.

I nod and open up. He pulls the trigger and beer floods into my mouth quicker than I can swallow it down. I choke and sputter until I get the hang of it.

Just as I feel like I might pass out from the blood rushing my head, the guys let me down, setting me on my feet.

Suddenly, I realize why people do this. The beer I drank feels like it has an instant effect. My head spins and my eyes blur.

River grabs me up in a bear hug and spins me around, cheering. When he puts my feet on the ground, I wander off to the privacy fence and release every last drop of beer from my body.

"Oh," Dave says. I can tell by his muffled tone that he's covering his mouth.

When my stomach is emptied, I walk back over to them and hold out my hand. "I'm Jovi."

"Dave," he says, shaking my hand.

"Thanks for the use of your keg and I'm sorry about barfing in your yard, but I think I'm going to go. I'm not feeling very well." Without waiting for a word from him, I walk back through the house and out to the car.

River comes chasing me out. "Are you okay?"

I nod while rubbing my head. "You really shouldn't have spun me around. I was already dizzy."

He lets out a small, embarrassed laugh, realizing his mistake. "I'm sorry. I wasn't thinking. Do you forgive me?"

I pull out the list and mark it off. "I guess. But now you have to tell me something."

He starts the car and starts off to our next destination. "What?"

"What are your plans when we get back home?" I don't look at him. I can't. I'm too nervous about his answer.

I can feel him watching me. "The first thing I'm going to do is get a driver's license."

I can't hold in my laugh.

"Then I'm going to drive over to your place and never leave. I hope you're okay with that. You're stuck with me." He grins making his eyes light up.

I feel something flutter in my chest, a feeling I've never

felt before. "Okay, but you're going to have to get a job. We can't both be unemployed."

His deep, sexy laugh fills the car. "We're a fucking mess, you know that?"

I nod with a smile. "I know. But I'd rather be a mess with you than put together with anyone else."

He leans over and kisses me breathless. "Let's go get this list done."

Soon after leaving the run down house, we're pulling up to some kind of amusement park. "What are we doing here? This isn't on the list."

He shuts off the car and removes his seatbelt. "I know, but bungee jump is." His eyes fill with excitement as he flashes me a wicked smile.

I clap my hands together as I bounce up and down in my seat. "I've always really wanted to do this but I was always too scared. It will be so much fun jumping together." I swing open the car door and climb out.

"Wait! Jovi, no!" He rushes to my side. "This one's just for you."

"Oh, no. If I go, you go!" I grab his hand and lead him to the gates.

We stand in line for what feels like three hours. But we're finally up next.

"Jovi, I seriously can't do this one." His voice is laced with nerves.

I turn to look at his pale face. "Are you afraid of heights?"

He swallows, a lump forming in his neck. "I can't do it. I'll tell ya what. How about neither of us do it and you just mark it off?"

"What? No! That's cheating! I have to do this. You don't."

"Really? You won't hate me for making you go alone?" His facial muscles go at ease with relief.

"You're not making me. I want to do this."

The man tells me to step forward to fit me with my harness. They go through an incredibly long list of technicalities before letting me walk over to the side where I jump. I spin around so I can look at River while I fall backward, wanting to take the love and excitement he makes me feel with me.

I hold my arms out at my side and slowly lean back, letting gravity take me over the edge. My stomach feels like it's still up on the platform, but I feel completely weightless, free. The wind whips my hair around me and makes me feel like I'm flying. My cheeks hurt from smiling and laughing. However, I'm not brave enough to open my eyes. I keep them squeezed shut. I don't need to see. I just need to feel.

I bounce around for a while, feeling like a cork that keeps getting pulled under water, but I'm finally pulled back up to the platform.

River is standing there with his hand covering his mouth, skin so pale it looks green.

"Oh, thank God!" He rushes over to me.

"What's the matter? Did you think I wasn't coming back or something?" I ask as the workers remove my harness.

"You were so fucking quiet, I thought something went wrong. Who jumps like that and doesn't scream?"

Finally I'm free from all the ropes and buckles so I take his hand and lead him away. "I didn't jump. I fell. Just like with us. I didn't jump into this," I motion between the two of us. "I fell."

He leans into me, pressing his lips to mine.

"Next!" I shout exhilarated as he pulls away, I'm feeling my old, timid self, transform day by day. I know that I am no longer the same person I was before the trip began.

It's nearing dinner time by the time we leave the amusement park. River drives us to the shore. "What are we doing here?" I ask as he turns the car off.

"Getting dinner."

"Here?" I point at the yacht.

"Yeah. I arranged it. I wanted to do something with you before we had to head back."

"Thank you. This is so sweet." He takes my hand in his and leads me up the ramp and onto the boat.

We sit at a small table on the elegant boat. A waiter serves us some wine while we slowly start drifting out into the ocean.

I take a sip and look across the table at River. I had no

idea he could be so sweet. We've spent a lot of time together this summer, but it wasn't spent "dating". Sure we would eat together, drink together, and spent pretty much all our time together, but we were doing so as friends. I never looked at him and felt like I was in a serious relationship with him because we were just having fun.

This, sitting together on this boat, being waited on as the sun sets in the sky, it feels like a date. Maybe he's trying to show me what really being together would be like. This is nice, but I don't need it. All I need is him by my side, making me laugh so hard my face hurts. I need to be under him every night while he shatters me into a million pieces. And most of all, I want to tell him I love him, but I don't know how to say the words.

"What are you thinking so hard about?" he asks me, his blue eyes meeting mine.

I shrug one shoulder. "Is this what dating you is like?"

He lets out a short laugh and shakes his head. "I don't really know. I've never really dated before."

I lean forward, needing to be closer to him for some reason. "You've never had a girlfriend?"

"No, not really. I mean, there have been girls, but none that I considered my girlfriend."

I look around the ocean and the sky. "So did you do anything like this for them?"

"Nope. Back in New York, I stuck to the basics. Dinner, drinks, maybe a movie or play, but nothing ever like this."

I smile, I can't help it, but hearing how special this really is for him, it means that much more to me.

It's completely dark by the time we are done eating. The waiter clears our plates and River stands, holding out his hand. "One more thing to check off that list today."

"What's that?" I take his hand as he leads me to the side of the boat.

"Look over there." He points to my right. I turn and look.

There are dozens of lit up paper lanterns floating through the air. I inhale from the beauty of it. It reminds me of the list. Number fifty says: *use a paper lantern to free something that's holding you back.*

I turn around to face him.

He's holding two lanterns. "Time to let Katie go."

I meet his eyes again, he's blurry through my tears. When I look down, he's holding out a lighter.

I reach for it, squeezing it hard in my hand. Can I do this? Can I let Katie go?

She's not holding me back, is she? She's pushing me forward. I never would have done any of this stuff this summer without her.

"I can't." I shake my head while my hot tears leak from my eyes.

"It's time, Jovi. She's gone. It's time you accept it. It will be the hardest thing you'll ever have to do, but once you do it, you'll feel the weight lift from your shoulders. You'll be free."

I have had this weight on my shoulders since she was taken. I've also had this knot in my stomach. Will letting her go make all that go away? Before I didn't want it to go away. I wanted the reminder. But maybe River is right. Maybe it's time to move on, try to heal. Katie wouldn't want me hurting.

I hold the lantern out as I strike the lighter. "I love you, Katie," I whisper as I hold the flame to the paper.

After a few minutes, the lantern fills and begins to float. Thinking about my friend, I watch it as long as I can, until it's no longer visible. I take a deep breath, and it soothes me. I do feel a little lighter.

I spin around to see River still holding his lantern. "What are you going to let go?"

He looks at me, pain reflecting in his eyes. "I'm letting go of all my anger and resentment."

"Anger and resentment about what?"

"About it all: my friend that overdosed, my mom getting taken from me, my dad who never wanted anything to do with me growing up, and my sister who I moved across the country to be closer to, only for her to be taken too."

The boat is pulling back up to the dock. I feel it shudder when the engine is shut off.

"Your sister? I thought you didn't have any siblings?"

His jaw is flexed like he's angry. "I may not have been completely honest with you."

I feel my defenses rise. "Why would you lie about having a sister?"

"Think about it, Jovi."

I lean against the railing of the boat and think over all of our conversations. I come up empty handed until my dreams of Katie pop into my head: her mom and dad fighting. A guy named Josh asking for money. River's story about showing up asking his dad for money.

Then another memory pops into my head. One I hadn't thought about in years.

Katie falls onto her bed next to me. There is something wrong with her. She looks angry or sad or something.

"I know the secret, Jo."

"What secret?" I ask, suddenly intrigued.

"What my mom and dad were fighting about that day. Why things have been weird between them for a while now."

"What? What is it?"

Her eyes fall to her hands, watching as she twists her fingers together. "I have a half-brother."

I feel my eyes grow wide. "What?"

She nods. "My dad got some lady pregnant before he and my mom got together. He gave her money to get rid of it. Apparently, he went all this time not knowing that she never did. She had the baby. I have a half-brother out there. Can you believe it?" Her eyes are wide, excited and yet, still completely unsure.

"Oh my God. This is crazy!"

"I know. His name is Josh. He's the guy that showed up

asking for money. My dad was so shocked when he showed up at the house, he turned him away before we came home. I guess he got in contact with his old flame and found out that she kept the baby. My dad broke the news to my mom over lunch that day and she stormed out. That's why they were fighting."

I'm in shock right now. Mary and George had always seemed like the perfect couple to me. Up until recently that is. But I never imagined George having a secret love child.

"So what now? What's going to happen?"

She shrugs. "I don't know. My dad finally told me about it all. He asked if I wanted to meet him, but I don't know if I can."

"Why? He's your brother."

"This whole thing has caused so much grief with us. It's like we're not even the same family anymore."

I pull her in for a hug, rubbing her back. "That's not his fault, Katie. He's innocent in all this. He didn't have a dad growing up, then he shows up and gets turned away. Can you imagine what he must be thinking right now?"

She pulls back. "I just need time to get used to the fact that I have a brother out there. But, you know, you're right. I'll call him soon and set up a time to meet."

I nod. "I completely understand. It's a lot to take in. Call him, when you're ready."

"Jovi," River's voice pulls me away from my memory.

I shake my head. "River, what's your middle name?"

He flexes his jaw before saying, "River is my middle name."

I cover my mouth with my hand as tears fill my eyes. "Josh?"

He nods, tears filling his own eyes, but he doesn't let them fall.

15

Time to run

My feet start backing away from him cn their own. "I don't understand."

"Please, just let me explain." He steps closer to me, but I step away.

"You've been *lying* to me. This whole time?" My voice is high pitched and I feel betrayed. I turn away. I can't look at him.

Anger floods over me and I turn back. "I've told you things I've never told another person, and you couldn't even tell me your real name?" I'm not sure which is stronger: anger or hurt.

He shakes his head as guilt and shame wash over his face. "It's not like that, Jovi. I swear. I wanted to tell you, I did. But I knew if I told you who I really was while you were still hurting with everything so raw, you'd just see Katie, and that would make you hurt worse."

"No. You don't get to tell me anything anymore. You had your chance. You don't know how I would've reacted. You didn't even give me the chance. You just assumed it would be better for me if you lied." I let out a laugh. "Well, that's the last time. Find your own way home." I turn and walk off the boat.

When I get to the car, I climb behind the wheel. I look up to see him leaning against the railing, hanging his head.

He looks so broken and part of me breaks a little. *No, I can't feel sorry for him. He's lied to me for three months!*

I back out as quickly as I can. I have to get back to the apartment and pack my things. I'm going home.

I GET my things from the apartment we've been staying in, but I don't make it out of town. My eyes are leaking tears so quickly, I can't see to drive. I stop at the first motel I find and rent a room for the night.

I fall down onto the bed and curl into a ball. I can't believe this. River is Josh – Katie's *brother*. The brother she didn't know she had until a few years ago. How could I have not put this together? I feel so stupid. I mean, it's not like I ever saw a picture of him. I remember her irritated laugh when she would show me all the pictures she had taken on her trips to see him. He always had a way of ducking out of the picture, or covering his face at the last second.

This makes me realize that I've had more of her than I originally thought. I thought all I had was this list and her ashes around my neck, but I've had her brother this whole time. The same blood that ran through her veins runs through his.

I hate myself for running from him, but I need time to think. He lied to me. He could have told me, but instead he chose to keep me in the dark.

I dry my eyes and step into the shower. I need to wash this day from my mind. As I lather up, the memories of my summer wash over me and my heart longs for him. I'm completely fucking addicted. He owns me, even my heart knows it. But I can't just go running back. I need to wrap my head around this. All of it, not just his lies.

When I get out of the shower, I sit on the bed and hold my phone in my hands, debating on calling George. He's the only one who can give me the truth. I need the truth to make my decision.

I hit the send button and the phone rings. As I'm sure it's going to go to voicemail, he answers. "Hello?"

"Mr. Hansen?" I nearly whisper.

"Jovi?" I can hear the concern in his voice.

I nod while wiping away tears that are falling on their own. "Yeah. It's me."

"What's wrong? Where have you been?"

I take a deep breath. "I've been in Miami. I took Katie's trip."

"Oh." I can hear the hurt from hearing her name lacing his words. "Well, is there something I can do for you?"

"Yes, actually. You can tell me about Josh."

"Josh? My son, Josh?"

"That's the one." I stand and start pacing the floor.

"What is it that you want to know?" He sighs.

"Everything," I breathe out. "I remember the fight. The one you and Mary had in the kitchen that day. And Katie told me some things, but I'd just like to hear it all from you."

He clears his throat and at first I think he may not answer but then he speaks. "Well, back when I first started my company, I went to a seminar in New York. After a day of classes, me and my partner went out, and I met some-one." He takes a long breath. "We had several drinks and one thing led to another and…well, you know."

Feeling slightly hysterical, I want to laugh because he can't just come out and say they had sex, but I don't. "Okay, what happened after that? I was told you paid her to get rid of the baby."

"Before I left to come back home, we exchanged numbers. A couple of months later, I got a call. She was pregnant. I had just met Mary and I was head over heels in love. I didn't want to let this woman I had a one-night stand with ruin my plans. I hadn't known Mary long, but I knew she was the one I wanted. So…we talked and she decided to get rid of the baby. She said she couldn't afford to do it on her own. She was living with one of her friends, and was only working part time. I told her I would wire her the money if she wanted. She accepted and I assumed she got it done. I never heard from her again."

"So when did you find out?"

"Not until fifteen years later when he showed up on my doorstep!"

"And you turned him away?"

I hear the shaky breath he takes even though the phone. "I did. It wasn't my finest hour, but I didn't know what else to do. I didn't want to believe him, but he looked just like me. Same blond hair, same blue eyes. I knew he was mine the second my eyes landed on him, but I didn't want to believe it. I didn't want to think about the problems it would cause in my family. So, yes, I turned him away."

I hear glass clanking together, like he's pouring a drink. I can see him now, in his home office, pacing the floor with a glass of scotch in his hand.

"I didn't want Mary and Kate to see him and ask questions. Not because I didn't want them to know, but because I needed the truth for myself first. It took me about a week, but I finally found her number. I called and she told me everything. She said she couldn't go through with it. It damn near crippled me because this whole time, I had a son out there that thought I didn't want him, and then I went and turned him away."

"And then what?" Tears are still leaking from my eyes and I don't even know why anymore.

"Well, then I told Mary. She was mad. She thought I had known the whole time, that I kept it from her, and she stormed out on me. When I got off work that day, I came home and that was the fight you girls heard. We fought about it for a long time. I wanted to contact him, give him whatever he needed, but Mary, she didn't even want to acknowledge that he existed. But finally, I told her that I was going to meet my son and there wasn't anything she could do about it. That's when I told Kate about the whole thing."

"That's when you guys went to New York to meet him."

"That's right. We made a trip to New York every year to visit. Josh and Kate talked weekly on the phone. He became family. I think he only moved out here because of his and Kate's relationship. They were close. Jovi, why are you wanting to know all of this?"

I decide to come clean. I should talk to someone about it. "He came to Miami with me. I didn't know who he was. I met him at your house the day of the funeral. He told me his name was River."

"I see. Now you feel like you don't know him at all?"

"Exactly. I told him things that only Katie knew, and he didn't even tell me his real name. I love him, but can I excuse this?"

Talking to George is like talking to my own dad. He knows me better than I know myself because he knew me before I was me. He watched me grow from a small kid with scraped up knees to the woman I've become.

"Jovi, listen to me. Life is too short to hold grudges. Whatever Josh did, he's a good kid and I'm sure he has his reasons. I'm sure he was only trying to protect you. There comes a time when you have to ask yourself, is the lie he told so bad that he can't be forgiven? If you love him as you say, shouldn't you forgive him?"

I nod. "I should, but I don't know if I can. I will always be wondering what else he's lying about."

"You don't love him because of his name, Jovi. Love is blind. It will sneak up on you when you're least expecting it. You love him because of the way he makes you feel. That wasn't a lie."

He's right. Who cares what he wants me to call him. I love him. "You're right," I whisper, suddenly realizing how badly I've fucked this all up. "I have to go. I have to find him." I stand and grab my bag.

"Be careful. And please come by and see us soon. We miss you," George says.

"I will, I promise," I say before wiping my cheeks and hanging up the phone.

I toss my bag into the backseat of the car and rush over to the apartment. I left my key inside when I left in such a rush, so I pound on the door relentlessly, but he doesn't answer.

I stand on my tiptoes and peak into the frosted glass window on the top. The place is dark. He's gone.

It feels like my whole world comes crashing down on me. My chest hurts as I turn back for the car, admitting defeat. He's gone, and I'll be lucky if I ever see him again.

I don't have the strength to drive all the way across the country by myself. I can't do it. That will be entirely way too much time to think about how I fucked this up. I just want to run home and crawl into bed. I want to be surrounded by my things, my memories. I want to be some-place where I can talk to Katie, a place where I feel close to her.

Luckily, I rented the car from a nationwide company. I turn over the car and get a taxi to take me to the airport. The whole way there, my stomach is in knots. I temporarily forget about the problems I caused with River. All I can think about now is getting on a plane so soon after my best friend died on one.

I'm almost having a panic attack by the time the cab pulls up front. Without allowing myself any time to think about what I'm doing, I climb out of the cab and rush inside to buy a ticket home.

Home. That's my only thought right now.

I buy a ticket, but the next flight is booked, so I have to wait until tomorrow morning, but even that will get me home faster than driving. I walk through the airport completely drained. The stress of the day has worn on me more than any other. I'm exhausted, worried, stressed, lonely, and afraid. I can't even bother to lift my head. I walk through the airport hanging my head, watching the floor, trying not to let the fear overwhelm me. Trying not to remember the images on the screen that fateful day.

Suddenly, every hair on my body seems to stand on end and a tingling forms in my stomach. My heart begins pounding wildly, and I look up in confusion, not sure why my body is acting this way.

I see vibrant blue eyes staring back at me and a mess of blond hair. His eyes narrow on me as he flexes his jaw. He looks angry, and sad, but so fucking sexy. I want to forget all about our fight. I want to rush into his arms and ask him to never let me go, but I can't seem to make my feet work. I'm frozen in fear because I don't know if he will want me after the way I acted.

16
Becoming River

THE PHONE RINGS AS I'M PACKING MY BELONGINGS. "Hello?"

"Josh? It's Dad," the man on the other end of the line says.

A wave of shock rolls over me. "Dad?" I fall to the edge of my bed that's covered in piles of trash and clothes from my quick attempt at packing.

"How'a doin' Son?"

I wipe the unshed tears from my eyes. "Not so well. Mom's funeral was today."

I hear his ragged breathing over the phone. "I'm so sorry, Son. I wish I could've helped you. I didn't even know you existed when you showed up. What can I do?"

I shake my head like he can actually see me. "Nothing. There's nothing to do."

"Look, Josh. I want to get to know you. I want a relationship with you."

I laugh, but it doesn't sound right. "Oh, now you want a relationship? What about your family?"

"My daughter, Katie, your sister, wants to meet you."

"And your wife?" I question. I knew she was the whole problem all along.

"She's not happy about it, but she won't be a problem. However, she won't be coming along either."

"Coming along? You mean, you're coming here?" I'm surprised. I never expected to see him again.

"If that's okay with you."

"Yea—" I have to clear my throat because my emotions are thick right now. "Yeah, I'd like that."

"Alright. I'll arrange everything now." I can hear the smile on his face. It brings out a smile of my own.

"Okay, great." I move the phone away to hang up, but hear him call out.

"And Josh?"

"Yeah?"

"Thank you for giving me a chance."

"You're welcome," I say before hanging up the phone.

The following week, nerves are eating me alive while I walk to the hotel restaurant George asked me to meet him at. I walk through the elegant building and stop before they see me.

I move next to the wall, just so I can study them for a brief moment. George looks like a good dad to her. They are talking, completely carefree and laughing. Seeing him this way, makes me a little jealous that I never got that with him.

I push down the anger that bubbles up with that thought and force my feet to move.

I walk up to their table and George's smile grows. He stands and pulls me in for a hug, gently slapping my back. "I'm glad you made it, Son."

"I wouldn't miss this for the world."

He turns to face my sister. "Kate, this is your brother, Josh."

Her eyes look me up and down, squinting with bitterness and anger as she holds out her hand.

It seems awkward to shake the hand of a sister you just met, but I shake it anyway. "It's nice to meet you."

"We'll see," she answers.

"Please have a seat, Josh. I'm going to use the restroom and track down our waiter." He walks off with confidence rolling off his suit covered body.

I sit across from Kate. "How are you?"

She lifts a shoulder, letting it fall quickly as her blue eyes that match mine narrow in on me. "Not great, as you can probably imagine."

"Why not?"

"Since you showed your face at my house, my parents have done nothing but argue. My family might be splitting up because of you." Her tone is harsh and shrill.

I let my eyes fall to the table between us. "I'm sorry. It was never my intention to cause problems with your family."

"Why now? Why show up now?" Anger is etched on her round face. She looks so young and innocent. So much unlike me.

"My mom was sick. She was dying and we couldn't afford the experimental drug she needed. I knew I was grasping at straws, but I had to try. I wanted to save her." I hope she can hear the pain in my voice. She's my family now. The only family I have since my mom passed. I need her more than her young mind can realize.

"Your mom died?" Her voice has now softened as realization washes over her.

I nod.

"Do you have any other family?"

"Nope. It's just me," I say, tearing a paper napkin to shreds.

Her hand covers mine. "We're family."

And like that, she accepts me.

For the next three days, they stay in New York, and we spend every waking minute together. When they leave, we exchange numbers, promising to talk at least once a week.

When I first met her, I thought she was going to be the tough one to crack, but she opened up to me like nobody ever has. We talked about her school, her best friend that has the weirdest name I've ever heard, and what she plans for the future. I'm in awe of her. She's young and still thinks everything is within her reach, and with her daddy's money, it might be. But I make sure to keep my current living situation under wraps. They don't need to know that I'm homeless and living out of a tent.

I don't want them to think I want anything other than love and understanding from them. I don't want to be another person holding out their hand.

Over the years, Katie and George make the trip every year. Every year, I'm surprised by how much my little sister has grown.

We always try to do something fun and special. We go to baseball games, concerts, and plays. She's one of these typical teenage girls that is obsessed with selfies, so she's constantly trying to take my picture. I'm not big on pictures, so in every one, I find a way to hide my face. A giant foam finger covers my face in the picture from the baseball game, my hand covers my face at the play, and I hold a cup of beer over my face at the concert. After years of doing this, she's finally figured out not to take my picture.

But each and every time they come to see me, Katie begs me to move out to California. I always promise her I will think about it, but never seriously do. I'm lucky if I have a buck in my pocket on most days, and that won't get me across the country.

I don't think about it seriously until years later, after my friend Dalton dies, leaving me all his money. I have more money than I've ever seen in my life. And with him gone, the advertising business doesn't have the same appeal. I decide this part of my life is done. It's time to move on.

I move to California and Katie is beyond excited. When I get all my belongings settled into my apartment, I call her up and set up a time to meet. We have a lot to catch up on. We've talked a lot over the years, but I still feel like I don't really know her. I'm looking forward to spending many years becoming as close as a brother and sister can.

I'm sitting at an outside coffee shop when she runs up. "I'm so excited you're finally here!" she screeches.

I stand and she pulls me in for a hug. "I am too. Where's this best friend you wanted me to meet?"

She rolls her eyes. "She had to work. She's responsible and won't call in."

I laugh as we take our seats across from one another. "So completely unlike you in every way possible."

She points her finger at me. "Exactly."

The waitress comes over and takes her order. When she walks away, I ask, "so what's new?"

A wide smile covers her face. "I'm going to spend the summer in Miami," she cheers.

"Are you serious? You finally got me here and now *you're* leaving?" I'm just teasing with her. I love how free she is. Nothing holds her back.

"I'm sorry. I've been begging you to come for years. I didn't know you'd actually go for it once I planned a trip."

"Don't worry about it, Kate. I'm just messing with you."

I take a sip of my coffee. "So is that best friend of yours going with you?"

She shakes her head. "No, but I've been trying to talk her into it. I've been coming up with ways I can trick her into going." She offers up an evil grin.

I laugh and shake my head. "How can you trick someone into going to Miami?"

"I have my ways," she says in a teasing voice.

I laugh and shake my head at her. I can see she has grown up a lot in the few years I've known her, but she's also spoiled and gets everything she asks for, so I'm not surprised she thinks she can talk her friend into a trip she doesn't want.

"So, what are your plans?" Katie asks as she sips her coffee she was just handed.

I shrug. "I don't even know where to start. I'm finally settled in my apartment. I'm torn between finding a job or just spending some time to find myself, you know? I've only ever been in advertising. I never went to college. I don't really know where to start."

Her blue eyes grow wide while a smile slowly spreads across her face. "I have an idea."

I'm feeling a little nervous now. "What kind of idea?" I ask, fear drenching my words.

"An idea for you to find yourself, to get out there and see where you end up." She reaches into her purse and pulls out a tiny, red, spiraled notebook and a pen.

She opens the notebook and starts writing.

"What the hell are you doing?"

Without looking up at me, she says, "I'm making you a bucket list."

I laugh. "A bucket list? Really? How is that supposed to help me discover myself?"

She looks up at me with some kind of knowing smile. "It's worth a shot, right?"

I wave her on. "Why not?"

We sit and have an easy conversation while she writes things down on my list. When she stands to leave, she slides over the notebook.

"The next time I see you, you better have this with you so I can see what you've managed to check off."

I grab it and slide it into my pocket. "Yes, Ma'am."

She pulls me in for a hug. "See you in three months, bro." She lightly punches me on the shoulder as she pulls away.

"When does your plane leave?"

"Five A.M. Saturday. I'm spending the day with Jovi tomorrow." She grabs her purse and runs away as quickly as she appeared.

Once she is no longer in my line of sight, I turn and walk in the opposite direction.

17

Happily Ever After?

I'M STOCK STILL, WATCHING AS HE WATCHES ME. HE LOOKS perfect as he stands there, bag hanging from his strong shoulder. His hair is disheveled and his jaw is cocked, his blue eyes are darkening as he watches me intently. This look of brooding makes him look dark and sexy. I hold the strap on my shoulder even tighter, waiting for what's sure to come.

He slowly starts moving towards me, and with each step, my heart pounds harder. My legs feel weak, like they are going to buckle at any minute. And my stomach is doing flips, filled with nerves about how this meeting will go. All I pray for is that he forgives me. I love him, and I'm ready to say it.

"What are you doing here?" I ask him, barely above a whisper when he closes the distance between us.

"Can we talk?" His voice is deep and rough as he looks down on me through his thick lashes.

I don't want to talk. I just want to feel his lips against mine. I don't care why he lied. All I care about is somewhere along the way, I fell in love with him.

I nod and he grabs my hand, leading me towards the hotel that is next to the airport. He doesn't stop or talk until he lets us into the room he had already rented for the night. He must have gotten a ticket on the same plane as me.

I let my bag slide from my shoulder onto the floor as I walk to sit on the foot of the bed.

I want to tell him everything that's been running through my head since I left him only a few hours ago, but I want to hear what he has to say.

When my eyes land on him. He's holding out a red, spiral-top notebook. "What's that?" I ask him.

He takes a step closer, holding out the notebook. I take it and open the cover, revealing Katie's handwriting. A shock jolts through me, burning a trail right to my heart.

She made him a list too.

"What is this?" I know, but I want him to say it.

"It's *my* list."

I look up at him briefly. "Katie made this for you?"

He nods slowly, eyes downcast.

I read over the first page. "*Kiss a girl on the dance floor?*" I quirk an eyebrow at him.

"That girl was you," he says as he moves to my side, taking the place next to me. "After her funeral, I needed to forget for a little while. I went to that bar intending on getting hammered so I could sleep, but then I saw you on that dance floor and it was like she was giving me a sign. I knew I had to do this list."

"Help someone who's grieving?"

He nods once. "That was also you."

"Meet me on the beach?" I look over at him suddenly realizing. "When did she make this list?"

His Adam's apple bobs in his throat. "Two days before her crash."

"That is the day she wanted me to go with her to meet *you.*"

He nods. "I had been hearing about you since the first time I met her. I was practically in love with you before we met."

My eyes fall back to his list. *"Meet me on the beach."* This is on my list too.

"I think she was trying to set us up. She told me that she was trying to trick you into going to Miami with her. It wasn't until I saw your list that I put two and two together. Since we couldn't meet that day, she was going to trick us into meeting in Miami."

My heart begins hurting all over again as I look at his list. *Kiss a girl on the dance floor,* did she set all this up? Was she hoping I would just happen to go to the same club to dance in public and we would meet?

"Did you go there looking for me?" I finally allow myself to look up at him.

"Not exactly. I mean, after you kissed me and walked away, I knew I had to find you again. I had no idea I'd run into you that night, but I'm glad I did." He moves to his knees on the floor in front of me. "Don't you see, Jovi? Katie *wanted* this. She knew we were meant to be together."

Part of me wants to give in, to believe him, but then I remember why I'm hurting. "But all of this is built on lies. Why didn't you tell me who you were?"

His hands land on my cheeks softly, forcing me to look at him, to see all the love and pain he holds within himself. "I couldn't. I knew if I told you she was my sister, that would cause you to run. I wanted you to see me for me, not just Katie's brother. I didn't want you to feel more pain from looking at me, I wanted to take that away from you. I wanted you to be free, not held back. I wanted you to let your guard down. And you did. You did all of those things. You checked everything off your list."

"There *is* still one thing on my list," I whisper.

Lines appear on his forehead as his hands fall from my face. "There is?"

I nod as I lean over and pull the list from my bag. I flip to the first page and show him.

"*Fall in love,*" he reads before he slumps back, looking defeated. His eyes fall to the floor as his jaw tics.

"Do you have a pen?" I smile as I'm saying the words.

He looks back up at me before his lips crash against mine. His fingers tangle into my hair, pulling me closer. A tingling sensation forms in the pit of my stomach. It lights every nerve ending as it spreads through me like wildfire, completely consuming me.

I don't know how he got to me, but he did. And he buried himself so deep inside my heart, there's no way he's ever leaving it. He went from a stranger who annoyed the fuck out of me, to becoming someone I love and long for.

He pulls away quickly.

"What are you doing?" I ask in a rush.

He pulls a pen from his pocket and hands it over to me.

I smile as I take it. Placing the pen to the paper, I slash through the last item on my list. I did it. I fell in love with my best friend's half-brother. And it's all because of her. She knew what I needed better than I did. She knew my heart when I didn't.

Before I remove the pen from the notebook, River's mouth is back on mine as he covers my body with his.

His hands travel from my face to my neck while I wrap my arms around him. I need to feel him against me. I lie back on the bed, pulling him up my body as I do so. He settles between my legs, pressing himself against my aching sex.

A whimper leaves me and I feel him twitch against me

He gets up to his knees and yanks his shirt off as I pull my shirt away. He's towering over me, pushing and pulling clothes from his body. When he's down to nothing but his white boxer-briefs that highlight the V between his hips, he lowers himself against my body again, eyes darkening and locked on mine like an animal stalking its prey.

His body is hard as it covers mine. His mouth trailing over my heated flesh teases me and causes my body to break out in goosebumps. His big hands firmly slide down my stomach, to my hips where he pushes my shorts down my thighs.

My hands are just as greedy as they tug down his boxers until his hard cock springs free and stands at attention.

When we're both completely bare for the other, he lays me back down, taking his place on top of me.

"I love you, Jovi," he whispers against my lips.

"I love you too, River." When the words leave my mouth, he rears back and slams into me, making me call out.

He grinds against me, making every muscle in my body tense as my orgasm rises. I'm quivering with need as he slowly brings all our shattered pieces together, forming one picture perfect future together.

We're not taking our time with one another. We can't. This is hard and fast, our bodies automatic response to one another.

It's a primal need deep inside us to completely fucking own the one we love. It's bone deep. It can't be ignored because it's not something we chose. We may both be broken beyond repair with all the loss and hurt we've dealt with in our lives, but we find relief in each other. We found love: an earth shattering, take you over, explosive kind of love. Something that can't be ignored no matter how hard we try. I can't run from it. I can't hide from it. It consumes me. It completely fucking shatters me.

He thrusts into me deep and hard. I'm calling out, he's breathing erratically and the room is filled with the sounds of our calls of passion, as we both find our release together. My nails bite into his back as his hands hold my hips tightly. He shudders as he pushes into me one last time before he slows and comes to a stop on top of me.

He leans back so he can look into my eyes. "You did it."

I wipe away a bead of sweat that's forming on his brow. "I did what?"

"You finished the list. What are you going to do now?"

I smile. "Help you finish yours."

Our lips crash together as our tongues swirl around, giving, taking, loving.

Katie knew what she was doing when she made us those lists. I can only hope she's smiling down on us right now, happy that she got her way again.

I know a part of me will miss Katie the rest of my life, but she gave me so much. She taught me how to let go of what society deems acceptable. She taught me to laugh and have fun, how to put myself out there and accept the consequences. She gave me friends, life lessons that I will use every day, and she gave me River. Strong, wild and free, River.

He helped me in more ways than I thought possible. He helped me let go of Katie. He showed me what it was like to love and be loved. He helped me finish my list. And if I know one thing, and one thing only, it is that I will help him finish his.

Josh's Bucket List

1. Kiss a girl on the dance floor
2. Take a chance
3. Help someone who's grieving
4. Join me on the beach
5. Meet Jovi
6. Fall in love
7. Let go of something that's hurting you
8. Conquer a fear
9. Get married
10. Live happily ever after

Epilogue
Six Months Later...

"Jovi, I can't do this." I shake my head vigorously as she leads me up the side of the mountain.

"It's okay. Just don't look down."

Her telling me not to look down does the exact opposite. I look down. My head starts spinning and all I can hear is my heart hammering away. It feels like my eyes cross and I fall to my knees.

She spins around and tilts her head to the side. "You looked down, didn't you?"

I nod, unable to talk. There is a lump in my throat that is blocking air and my voice.

She walks the couple steps back to me and sits down on the dirt trail at my side. "We don't have to do this, you know?"

I'm finally able to swallow the excess salvia in my mouth as I nod my head. "Yes, I do. It's on the list: conquer a fear. Heights is my fear— we're doing this."

"Okay, well why don't we just hang here for a minute and catch our breath. Look at that view." A breathtaking smile covers her face. It's so bright it lights up her dark brown eyes. She's come a long way since we got back from our trip. She's completely free. She's let go of everything that had been holding her back, and she's blossomed into a beautiful woman who isn't held back by anything. She's learned how to let things go and move on. She's taking chances and doing anything and everything she wants to do. She doesn't pretend to be anyone else. She's just her and if you don't like it, you can fuck off. She no longer hides herself away.

Seeing her like this, makes me want her more every day. She's completely fucking breathtaking as she stares out over the mountain. Her chest is rising and falling quickly with her heavy breathing from the hike. The look in her eyes drives me crazy. I want her. Every day, just me and her.

I reach out and run my fingertips down her arm. She quickly looks over at me with a smile. "Are you ready?"

"Yeah, I'm ready." Just sitting here, watching her, has calmed my nerves. She always does this for me. She brings me back from whatever cliff I'm on.

There is more to this than just marking this one thing off the list. I can't wait to get to the top.

I stand and pull her up with me. I keep her hand in mine as we continue our way up the mountain trail.

It takes us another hour, but we've finally made it. I stop some way from the edge and bend over with my hands on my knees while I try catching my breath, but she doesn't. She races right to the edge to peer over.

She's completely fearless and free. I watch her from my position as she holds her arms out at her side, like she's opening herself up for the world to see.

My heart pounds away in my chest. It's time.

I stand up right and walk over to the edge.

She looks up at me with a wide smile. "You did it! Cross it off."

I bring her against my chest and kiss her. Her soft lips press against mine and I know what I'm about to do it right.

When I pull away, I look deeply into her eyes. The fact that I'm standing on the edge of a cliff doesn't even register. I'm not afraid because I have her in my arms. Our hearts beat together as one as I stare into her beautiful soul.

"Jovi, will you marry me?"

Her mouth drops open before it's replaced with a wide smile. Her dark eyes only seem to burn brighter. "Yes," she nearly whispers with a nod of her head.

I crush her lips with my own, feeling, tasting, loving. She's mine and will be for the rest of my life.

When I pull away, I take the ring from my pocket and show it to her. She gasps and covers her mouth.

I know I've already proposed, but I drop to my knee

anyway as I take the ring from the box. "Jovi, you're everything I ever wanted in life. I know you think I saved you in some way, but really it was you who saved me. I've been broken for so long now, I didn't think I would ever be put back together. But…" I slide the ring onto her finger. "as it turns out, the pieces I was missing were yours."

She drops down to her knees in front of me and wraps her arms around my neck as she presses her lips to mine. I tangle my fingers into her hair and pull her as close as I can get her.

Here we are, kneeling on the side of a cliff, inches from falling to our deaths, and all I can think about is making her mine. I feel like I'm on the top of the world right now, and nothing can bring me down.

WE'RE WALKING hand in hand down the trail. The wind blows slightly, cooling our overheated skin. We're quiet as we're walking, just letting nature go on around us. It's relaxing, like we're the only two people left on the planet, and I'd be completely okay with that.

She squeezes my hand. "Are you ready to go back to work tomorrow?"

I shrug. "I'm excited to see what I can accomplish with this new advertising company. What about you? Are you looking forward to starting college?"

She smiles wide. "I am. I can't wait to become a grief counselor."

My feet stop moving on their own. "You've decided?"

She turns towards me, her smile still in place. "I have. I think it only makes sense, don't you?"

I can't help the grin that appears as I pull her closer to me. "I think it makes perfect sense." I pull her against my chest, my lips landing on hers.

She breaks away and looks into my eyes. "You've helped me so much since losing Katie. I want to do that for someone else."

I brush away a fallen hair from her face before placing my hand softly against her cheek. "I love you, Jovi."

Her hand covers mine like she never wants it to leave. "I love you too, River."

The End

Chapter One — Alexis

My phone rings, drawing my attention away from the book I'm reading. I mark the page with my makeshift bookmark and set the book down on my bed as I slowly reach for the phone, not in any hurry to answer it. In my experience, my phone ringing is never a good thing.

I roll my eyes when I see it's my mother's name on the screen. I hold the phone in my hands, deciding whether or not to answer it. Realizing that she won't stop calling if I don't, I finally pick up.

"Hello?"

"Alexis, why haven't you called? I've left you three

messages." Her voice is dripping with disappointment and annoyance.

I pet my cat, Smoky, to distract myself. "I'm sorry. I've just been busy working."

I swear I can hear her eyes rolling. "Well you don't have to lie. I know that meaningless job you have doesn't keep you *that* busy."

Hearing her call my job meaningless for the hundredth time annoys me to no end. "Is there something you need?" I clip out.

"You need to come home. Your sister's engagement dinner is this weekend and you WILL attend." She clearly wants to say more about my attitude, but restrains herself. She doesn't want to push me right now because she needs something from me.

"And why do I need to be there for that?" Smoky jumps off my lap and darts for the bedroom door, probably scared from hearing my mother's shrill voice.

"It is a very public affair and the whole family needs to be involved. Why do you have to be so selfish?"

"I'm really busy this weekend. I don't know if I can make it on such short notice." I'm playing with her now, only to stall the anxiety that rises in my chest at the thought of going home.

"I've been leaving you messages for weeks regarding this weekend. Don't act like I didn't give you enough notice. Don't make me send your father up there. You know I will," she threatens.

"Fine, Mom."

"Thank you. Be here by dinner on Friday. The engagement dinner is Saturday night and then we will have a family brunch Sunday morning." I can hear the excitement in her voice. It's not excitement about finally seeing her daughter again, though; she is only excited because she got her way.

"See you this weekend, Mom." I hurriedly hang up the phone before she can insult me further by telling me to get a more presentable haircut, or to make sure my nails are done properly.

It has been six years since I have been home, and I still have no desire to go back.

Before my mind wanders to the reason I ran away in the first place, I pull back my blankets and slide underneath them.

Morning comes way too quickly — as is always the case when something dreadful lies in wait at the end of the day. Smoky's big green eyes are the first thing I see when I wake, only an inch away from my own.

This used to scare the shit out of me, but I've gotten used to it. I smile and rub his head before pulling him against my chest.

"Good morning, Smoky. Let me guess, you're hungry."

He responds with a meow that I assume means *yes*.

His soft fur tickles my nose and makes me laugh. "Okay, let's get you some breakfast."

I am absolutely terrified of going home. So, naturally, the day passes by unusually quickly.

My phone rings while I'm packing my bag, and I answer it wearily.

"Hello?"

"Hey, Alex. I got your message and I don't mind stopping by to feed Smoky for you this weekend." It's Jeff.

A long breath escapes my lips. "Thank you so much. I will make it up to you, I promise. Do you still have your key?"

"Yeah, I have it. And don't worry about making it up to me. I like it when you owe me." His tone is teasing, but I don't doubt that he does. "What are you going out of town for anyway?"

"My mother," I practically spit out.

"Ahhh, I see. Need me to show up and bail you out?"

I laugh. "I wish you could. I have a feeling she isn't letting me go before Sunday afternoon." I throw myself down across my bed and stare up at the white ceiling tiles. "I appreciate this, you know."

"It's not a problem. But Sunday night, you're mine." His voice grows thick and is laced with all sorts of dirty things.

"Deal," I say, turning over onto my stomach. Smoky is across the room jumping up and down, trying to get the curtain.

"Quit that," I tell him, tossing a small decorative pillow towards him. Unfortunately, he knows that I would never actually hit him, so he is unfazed by the pillow.

I roll my eyes but leave him alone. Who am I to stop his fun?

"I need to go, Alex. I have to get back to work. Call me this weekend if you need me."

"I will. Thank you, again."

"You will be doing plenty of that on Sunday," he teases before hanging up.

I fear that he is getting too serious.

We are just friends.

Friends that hook up because we're both too fucked up for anyone else.

I'm afraid we may have taken our friendship too far.

I am not in a position to be in a relationship, which is part of the reason we started this thing we're doing. It's been a long time since my last relationship.

A loud noise interrupts my thoughts. I jump and turn toward the sound to find that Smoky has finally gotten the curtain and managed to pull the whole rod down from the wall.

"Smoky, you're lucky you're so cute," I smile and shake my head at him.

I finish packing and am on the road by two in the afternoon, with a tankful of gas and a passenger seat stocked with Red Bull and Pringles.

My heart pounds against my chest as I pull onto the freeway.

"I can do this. If I'm careful, I can probably get through the whole weekend without even seeing him," I tell myself, trying to wrestle my racing heart back under control. My eyes flash to the passenger seat. "Maybe Red Bull wasn't a good idea."

In an attempt to drown out any thoughts, I dig my copy of Blink-182's self-titled album out of the glove box and slide it into my CD player. Their music always soothes me, especially when the volume is cranked all the way up.

Two and a half hours later, I see my exit. The volume on my radio automatically lowers as I exit the interstate and slow the car down.

"Don't get quiet on me now! I need you more than ever," I say, turning the dial back up.

Hanging a right off of the ramp, I cruise as slowly as possible without appearing suspicious until I pass the sign on the side of the road that reads, *Welcome to Cumming*. The sign fills me with memories faster than I can stop them.

Striker is sitting on the ground smoking a cigarette while I make adjustments to our welcome sign.

"How's it look from back there?" I ask him.

"It looks like a giant dick," he answers.

I turn and look over my shoulder at him before laughing at the stupid grin on his face.

He has his hood pulled up, shadowing all but his lips.

"Okay, I think I'm done." I take a few steps back to admire my handiwork.

The sign that previously said, Welcome to Cumming *now reads* Thanks for Cumming. *Below these words, a massive spray-painted dick is ejaculating onto the state bird.*

He walks up behind me and my back presses into his strong chest. The contact automatically stirs up all the feelings that I've been trying to hold back.

"I knew that fucked-up head of yours could come up with something." The amusement in his voice is clear.

I turn and look up at him. His green eyes light up and remain locked on mine. I love his eyes. They remind me of laying in the shaded grass on a hot summer day. I don't want to pull my eyes away from his, but instead end up watching as he pulls his bottom lip into his mouth and releases it. My eyes are transfixed on his moist lips.

"Lex, I'm going to kiss you now." His eyes watch me intently.

Heat creeps up into my cheeks. "Okay." I nod, watching his jaw twitch.

He moves so slowly that I wonder if he's changed his mind. He places his hands on either side of my face, maintaining his intense gaze. I moisten my lips in preparation for the kiss, and close my eyes. After a pause that feels like forever, his soft lips finally touch against mine.

It's like an electric shock to my body. They move slowly with my own lips, and all I want to do is devour him. I have dreamt about this kiss for years. Why is he finally giving into me now?

I lift my hands and hang onto his jacket, pulling him closer. His scent teases me. I want nothing more than for him to throw me down in the grass and show me what else that mouth is capable of.

He doesn't, though. Instead, he pulls away. His hands are still on my face and he leans his forehead against mine. "I've been waiting years to do that," he whispers into the darkness.

I'm breathless. I want to ask him why he waited so long. I want to know if this is going to change things for us. But I don't ask him any of that. I just close my eyes, feeling his heat sink into me, and relive our passionate, utterly perfect first kiss. The kiss that makes me know, beyond a shadow of a doubt, that I am in love with Striker Murphy.

Seeing that sign brings back everything I felt that night and everything I ran away from six years ago. I shake my head to clear the thoughts and pull out the emergency pack of cigarettes that's tucked into the side pocket of my purse. They have been sparsely used lately, only in times of extreme stress, but I have a feeling that I will have burnt through the entire pack by the end of this weekend.

I light the cigarette and take a long drag — instantly feeling some of the tension leave my body. The smoke flows out of the small crack in my window, where it swirls and fades away into the trees.

The bump as my car crosses the railroad track signals that I have reached the edge of town. There is no turning back. A wave of anxiety rises in my chest and I take another long drag of my cigarette, hoping to kill the feelings.

Continuing on, I keep my eyes straight ahead and avoid looking at the houses and buildings – each of which is home to some long-forgotten, often painful memory.

"Just drive. Don't look around, and don't stop until you get where you're going," I tell myself.

A siren blares behind me, followed by a flash of red and blue, and it is no longer possible to *just drive*.

My eyes move to the rearview mirror. "Fuck! Already?"

I flick my cigarette out of the window and slowly pull to the side of the road.

An old man exits the vehicle and walks up to the side of my car, adjusting the belt around his large waist. He taps on the window and I roll it down the rest of the way.

"Alexis Grant, I'll be damned. I never thought I'd see the day."

"Hi, Officer Willis. How are you on this lovely day?" I say politely with my eyes straight ahead, refusing to look at him. This old geezer has had it out for me ever since I was twelve-years-old. Ever since he suspected me and Striker of stealing the police car he left the keys in. He never could prove it was us — especially since it now resides at the bottom of the town lake.

"Skip the pleasantries, Grant. What do you think you're doing back here?" He smooths down his thick black and gray mustache.

Who does he think he is? He doesn't own this town. I can come here anytime I damn well please. I turn towards him in anger and say, "I'm here for my sister's engagement dinner. Is that okay with you? Or have you become the town mayor since I left?"

His response is a low grunt. "How long you staying?"

"Just the weekend, and then I promise I will be out of your hair," I say with my hands in the air, like I'm throwing in the towel. If he wants this town so bad, he can have it. I don't even *want* to be here, and yet here I am, already being harassed by the town sheriff.

"Let me know when you leave, I'll escort you out… again." He turns to walk away, but stops. "And don't even think about meeting up with Murphy. He's been in enough trouble all on his own." Now that he thinks he's gotten the last word, he resumes walking to his car.

"Okay, Barney." It slips out of my mouth before I can stop myself.

The words stop him in his tracks. He comes back to me and leans down, resting his hands on the side of my car. "What did you call me?"

I stifle back a laugh. "I didn't call you anything. Maybe it's time you retire, Officer Willis. It's dangerous for a man of the law to be going senile." My laughter is contained, but I can't hold back my smile.

"That's it, step out of the car." He opens my door for me.

All humor is gone now. "What? Why?" I reach out and close the door, refusing to move.

He stands up straight. "You're under arrest. Now, get out."

"For what?" I yell back, a little too loudly.

It takes him a minute to think of a good answer. "Obstruction of justice. Now, if you don't get out of that car it will also be for resisting arrest."

"Are you serious? I've barely made it twenty feet into town and you're going to arrest me? If I didn't know any better, I would say you're still holding a grudge against me. Even though we both know that I had nothing to do with your old police cruiser."

That clearly struck a nerve. The police cruiser, which I may or may not have sunk, was a gift from the town — a reward for his many years of dedicated service.

He points his finger at me angrily. "We both know that you and Murphy stole that cruiser. Get out of the car, NOW!"

I take a deep breath before grabbing my purse and opening my door.

The handcuffs are securely around my wrists before I

can even think of anything else to harass him about, and he yanks my purse from me.

I calmly head to the police cruiser and take a seat in the back while he stands outside and calls a wrecker to pick up my car.

My dad is going to have a field day with this one.

Acknowledgments

Wow! Here we are again! I can't believe this is my seventh time writing acknowledgements! I never expected to make it this far. I thought I would be laughed out of every digital bookstore, never seriously thinking that anyone would like my stories. You guys surprise me every day! The amount of time you put into reading, reviewing, and sharing my work is nothing short of amazing. Thank you to all my readers for loving my books and allowing me to provide you with more!

To my editors, cover designer, and proofreaders, thank you for helping make this book awesome!

Always to my hubby. You drive me crazy, but I love you anyway. Thank you for pushing me to follow my dreams.

To my kids, I love you both so much. And, as usual, you probably shouldn't read this one either. Like, ever!!

To my parents, I love you guys. Thank you for raising me to believe that anything is possible.

To my best friend, Sarah, you're awesome. I have to admit, when I was writing this, I tried to think about how I would feel if I ever lost you. Without a doubt, I would be fucking shattered. Thank you for kicking me in the ass when I need it. I love you!

To KG, you're awesome. You helped me so much with this book. You were there when I needed someone to bounce ideas off of, and you even named River. You're a great friend and a great author.

To my mother-in-law, Debbie, You've read all my books and push me to write more. I love that we have such a close relationship. I think of you as my own mother. Thanks for always being there for me. Love you!

To my betas, Jennifer and Dusty, thank you guys for reading, loving, and promoting my work! It seems the both of you can always cheer me up. I'm lucky to consider you two friends!

To Jennifer Jones, thank you so much for helping make this book better! I'm so glad we're becoming close!

A big thank you to Sarah Puckett. You not only did an amazing job voicing Jovi, but you also killed it with River. This book has reached so many more people because of the voice you gave to these characters.

Most of all, thank you to all the people who have dedicated their time to read, review, share, and promote this book.

Last but not least, my review group! You guys are so awesome. I love each and every one of you! Thanks for joining the group and taking this crazy ride with me! I asked you guys for your bucket lists, and you really let me have it!

Also by
K.B. Andrews

The Chance Series

A Chance At Forever

A Second Chance at Forever

Our Last Chance at Forever

One Last Chance at Forever

The No-Chance Series (Coming Soon)

Giving Up Our Chance at Forever

Fighting For Our Chance at Forever

Saving Our Chance at Forever

The Hope Series

Wrapped in Hope

Bound to Hope

Lost in Hope

<u>**Standalone Novels**</u>

Shattered (Also on Audible!)

Losing a Piece of Me (Also on Audible!)

Sweat

Feathers & Curls

About the Author

K.B. Andrews was born and raised in The Heartland where love and family values are just as important as going to church on Sunday. Marrying her childhood best friend—that she met on the first day of kindergarten—she believes in soulmates and love stories that have been written into the stars. She uses real life events as her inspiration to create stories that come to life on the page, that pull you in and hold you captive until the very end.